D1270178

Books by Dayton O. Hyde

Island of the Loons
The Major, the Poacher, and the Wonderful One-Trout River
One Summer in Montana

One Summer in Montana

One Summer in Montana

❖

DAYTON O. HYDE

Atheneum   1985   New York

Library of Congress Cataloging in Publication Data

Hyde, Dayton O.
One summer in Montana.

SUMMARY: A street tough hiding out in a rodeo in
Montana finds that it brings out his way with animals
and answers his needs for danger and romance.
[1. Rodeos—Fiction. 2. Montana—Fiction.
3. West (U.S.)—Fiction. I. Title.
PZ7.H9676On 1985 [Fic] 85-7961
ISBN 0-689-31144-3

Copyright © 1985 by Dayton O. Hyde
All rights reserved
Published simultaneously in Canada by
Collier Macmillan Canada, Inc.
Composition by Maryland Linotype, Baltimore, Maryland
Printed and bound by Fairfield Graphics,
Fairfield, Pennsylvania
Designed by Scott Chelius
First Edition

Acknowledgments

Paul Bond, who helped me down on my first top saddle bronc, Harry Rowell, who gave me my first job clowning and fighting brahma bulls, and Mel Lambert, who checked my memory for details.

To my friend Slim Pickens,
1919 to 1983.
One of the great personalities of rodeo,
a cowboy and an actor,
who never knew a stranger nor
failed to have time for a friend.

One Summer in Montana

The sandy-haired boy sat in the rider's seat in the cab of the big truck and ran the tiny map light over the road map spread across his knees, tracing the route the driver had crayoned in.

"Prairie City, Montana!" he said suddenly. "That's where I want to go, Mister!" Never been east of Oakland before, but Prairie City sounds like a place for a fresh start. A fresh start! You think life ever really gives anyone a second chance? I sure hope so. I don't mind tellin' you, when you picked me up along the highway back there in California, I was in trouble right up to here!"

chapter one

◈

The boy hadn't been in Prairie City ten minutes when he spotted trouble coming. Trouble with a capital T. He had just forked over his last six bits for a bowl of hot chili when he noticed five young locals, arms linked, moving shoulder-to-shoulder past the rodeo concession stand, forcing an oncoming knot of women and children to step off the boardwalk into the dusty street. He wished he were back in the air-conditioned cab of that big, brand-spanking-new 1947 Kenworth truck, safe and sound, hitching a ride north.

"Prairie City," the truck driver had said. "Tumbleweed capital of the world! Pretty quiet little town, except fer now, when the annual rodeo's on, and folks come in fer a hunnerd miles around t' celebrate the Fourth. Some good ranches around here. Might find yerself a job if yer interested."

When the truck stopped for the town's one traffic light, the boy stepped down. Now he knew it was a mistake, but

3

already the truck was working itself back up through its gears as it gained the summit of a distant hill.

The leader of the gang singled him out and dragged the rest to a halt while he sized up the stranger. Sensing this was no place for a loner on the run, the boy handed his bowl to an old man.

"Here, Mister! Take this. All of a sudden I ain't hungry!"

"Thankee, lad! Thankee!" the man called after him. He took the green plastic spoon in one palsied hand, only to have the bowl knocked to the ground as the gang shoved by.

"Sorry, Gramps," one of the gang apologized. "Let me help you, my good man." He picked up the fallen bowl, shoved it in the old man's face, then ran laughing after the others.

"You see them bib overalls?" the leader asked. "Thet's gotta be the hitchhiker I seen climbing down offen thet truck. Maybe we ought ta show him Prairie City's our own personal town."

"Bet he's just some punk farm kid from the Corn Belt," one of the gang said. "He ain't worth our time."

"What if he's just the first of more to come?" the leader said. "He gets on the phone an' tells some buddies there's a good thing goin' up north called Montana, an' a better thing called Prairie City. No two ways about it. There's five of us an' one of him. We're goin' ta show him we don't allow no mavericks joinin' our herd—onless they're heifers."

The boy, in worn overalls, tattered denim shirt with exploded elbows, and beat-up tennis shoes, ducked suddenly around the front of a parked car and lit out before the locals could get their cowboy boots untracked. Rolling under a moving livestock truck, he barely missed being flattened by the rear duals. Scrambling to his feet, he sprinted across a

4

dusty lot toward a carnival, pushed through a crowd, then leaped on the moving platform of the carousel, rode it half around and jumped off the far side as his pursuers piled into the startled spectators.

"Hey, you guys! Slow it down!" a deputy shouted. He moved toward the source of trouble, but the boys scattered.

Their quarry dashed through a sea of brown canvas tents, ropes, and stakes, then wheeled to get his bearings. Unused to the Montana air, his breath came in gasps, and he crowded his elbows tight against aching sides.

He heard boots pounding hard on dirt; someone was coming! He backed into the hot, musty envelope formed by two big tents butting up together. Lifting the canvas on one side, his hand met the groping trunk of an elephant; on the other side the way was blocked by three carnies asleep on a bed of hay. He stayed where he was, hoping the hay dust wouldn't make him sneeze.

He heard footsteps just outside his hiding place. The canvas trembled as someone tripped over a tent rope, cursed, and went on, searching out a way through the blind alleys, then giving up and going back the way he had come.

The boy left his hiding place and moved on. Ahead of him, behind one of the tents, some straw bales had been piled into a cave, and from the entrance, two small, dusty legs protruded. The boy grabbed at the ankles and extracted a small boy, blinking at the light as he clutched a cigarette.

"Divvy up!" his captor demanded, "or I'll call the fire marshal!"

"Aw, c'mon. Divvy up what? This here's just a butt I picked up. You ain't with the carnival; lemme alone."

He picked the boy up by the heels and shook him. Out fell a pack of Lucky Strikes, some small change, a folding knife, and a small, flat pry bar for jimmying windows. The tall boy scooped up the change, the cigarettes, and the knife, then dropped the kicking youngster and lost himself in the trembling sea of canvas.

"Ya know," the boy called after him as he retrieved his butt and took a drag, "it's getting to be a jungle around here."

The youth crept on hands and knees under the tent ropes until he could see out. Across the way, past the noisy world of the carnival, was the rodeo arena, its stands packed with spectators. Beyond a chain-link fence, he could see bucking chutes, roping pens, and clusters of horses and cowboys waiting their turn to compete.

It was all strange to him, and he watched in fascination as a chute gate swung open, towing a bareback bronc and rider out into the arena. The horse bucked in circles, kicking high behind, squealing and grunting every time its front feet hit the ground, while the rider's free hand cut circles in the air, and he kicked his feet toward the heavens, spurring as though a pot of prize money depended upon his ride.

"Hey." The youth grinned. "Now wouldn't I like to be able to ride like that!"

Once the whistle blew, two riders galloped in to sandwich the bronc between their horses. One cowboy leaned to loosen the flank strap, while the other reached to grab the rider by the far armpit, swinging him neatly from the horse's back to the ground.

"Tough luck for that cowboy," the announcer boomed. "The judges say he failed to spur the horse out of the chute, and so he draws a big goose egg. Folks, these cowboys pay entrance fees to compete, and when they don't win, all they get is the experience."

The cowboy stalked back toward the chute, shaking his head and kicking clods as though angry with himself.

The boy took in the lay of the land. He could see that the gang had regrouped and were leaning against the bed of a battered pickup truck, sharing a six-pack of beer. If only he could get to the other side of that chain-link fence, where the public was not allowed, he might be safe.

Trouble was, the guards at the gate allowed only contestants into the area behind the bucking chutes, checking for the red, white, and black numbered squares pinned to the cowboys' backs or their trouser legs. No way could he get past without a number. And yet he couldn't risk trying to go back the way he had come. That deputy sheriff had seen him running and might be edgy, checking ID's. The last thing he wanted was to get picked up for vagrancy and shipped back to California.

Near the tent village were public rest rooms. He watched as a contestant strode across the track to the men's room, laid his jeans jacket over the railing, opened the flimsy door and went inside. The number pinned to the jacket flapped enticingly in the breeze.

Using a cluster of horsemen as a screen, the boy left cover and moved to the fence, leaning on it as though waiting his turn. In seconds the number was in his pocket, safety pins and all. The cowboy came out, grabbed his jacket, swung it over one shoulder, and went off to the concession stands, while the youth took his place inside. Moments later, when he came out, the stolen number was pinned to his pants leg.

Towing a four-horse trailer, a pickup truck stopped on the track, and a cowboy got out to check his load. Quickly, the boy moved along the off side of the truck, grabbed a pair of western boots from the bed, stamped them on, replaced them with his worn sneakers, and was away before the cowboy could return to his cab.

Checking on the gang, he saw that they had spotted him. Clutching their beer bottles, they moved to overtake him. He hurried forward, heading toward the contestants' gate. He couldn't figure out why they were so persistent. Maybe they mistook him for someone else, figured from his clothing he was an easy mark. Or maybe they just didn't tolerate strangers on their turf. His eluding them seemed to have made them determined to stay on his trail.

The cowboy ahead of him had a foot in a walking cast, and the boy too affected a limp. Approaching the guards at the gate, he stopped and bent over to brush his pants cuff, giving the contestant ahead time to untie his horse from the fence and lead it through the gate. With the gate already open, he moved in behind the horse, keeping a wary eye on the horses's hind feet, afraid of getting kicked.

As he passed through, he glanced at a wristwatch, frowned as though late for an event, and flashed his leg number carelessly. The guards looked him over closely, but let him pass.

Behind him, three of the youths came together in a rush, but the steel gate slammed in their faces.

"Hey!" one of the guards snapped. "Cain't yuh read? Contestants only. Yuh want tuh see thiseer rodeo, go buy some tickets!"

For a moment it seemed as though the three were weighing their chances of rushing the guards, but instead they shot one more look at their quarry, took a fix on where he was headed, and moved on up the fence.

chapter two

❦

Putting as much distance as he could between himself and the fence, the lanky youth moved off over a dusty field of oak stubble, thronged with pickups, horse trailers, stock trucks, and recreational vehicles. Here and there contestants lounged about, resting up from the rigors of travel, outwardly relaxed, inwardly preoccupied with their upcoming events. Ahead of the boy, a roper stood idly by, mechanically throwing his loop over a set of real steer's horns stuck on a bale of hay, flipping the loop back off, recoiling his rope, shaking out a new loop, and throwing again.

Other cowboys played cards on tables made from blankets draped over hay bales. Bull riders leaned back against bull ropes, carefully rubbing in a dust of rosin, concentrating as though attention to detail might mean win or lose, life or death. The rodeo clown and bullfighter came out of his trailer dressing room, face white with greasepaint, blinked at the sunshine, and sloshed a basinful of milky wash water into the dust.

Behind the trailers, a pretty woman wearing a glittering, red-sequined riding outfit cantered a yellow horse in a lazy circle. Both hands locked on the tall, straight saddle horn, she practiced flying mounts and dismounts in lazy perfection.

Watching her spellbound, thinking he had never seen a sight more beautiful, the boy tripped over the outstretched legs of a heavy cowboy playing cards.

"Hey, watch it, kid!" the angry cowboy snarled from under his dusty black hat. He had a silver belt buckle covering part of his plump belly, in the center of which was a golden bucking horse with a ruby eye, and an inscription reading "World Champion All-Around Cowboy," the name "Ruff Burleigh," and a date some five years in the past.

"Sorry," the boy mumbled and got out of there.

Unaware of the trouble she had caused, the trick rider kept on with her practicing.

Riding toward him, the boy saw what he took to be the rodeo manager, a tall, handsome, silver-maned cowboy mounted on a flashy spotted horse. The man rode a saddle heavy with silver, and his chaps of ornately tooled leather bore the gold letters K.R. On a lesser figure the outfit would have seemed too rich, too ornate. The boy looked longingly at the silver and gold, wondering what a haul like that would bring in certain shady shops he knew about back home.

The rider loped on past the boy, his rigging creaking, glancing at the youth, but seeing him only as an obstacle to be skirted on the road. As he approached the arena fence, a gate swung open for him, and he was lost from view.

On the racetrack outside the chain-link fence, the youth

saw his enemies circling, keeping tabs on him, and the compound suddenly took on the aspect of a cage. Among the cowboys in big hats and blue jeans, his farm-style overalls made him stand out. Well, he'd better fix that. Ducking into an untended camp trailer, he came out moments later transformed. He had folded the top half of his overalls under, fastening them with a belt. He wore an ornate silver and orange western shirt, and a big, brown cowboy hat rode heavily on his ears, causing them to jut out at right angles, like wings. Whoever lived in that trailer must be a good-sized man.

In one hand he carried a pair of spurs, and as he sauntered over to a trash barrel and dumped in his rags, he adopted a rolling swagger. Leaning against a post, he tried to figure out how to put on the spurs.

Feeling eyes upon him, he looked up to see a cowboy his own age watching him curiously, but the youth got suddenly busy, turning away to climb up on the side of the corral to shoo some rodeo broncs from one holding pen to another. A chill ran through the boy. He wondered how long the cowboy had been watching him, and how much he had seen.

Slamming a gate behind the horses, the cowboy dropped back to the ground and strolled over as though to visit.

"Hullo," he said. "Guess we've never met. Name's Jimmy Richards. My dad's King Richards. He's furnishin' the stock fer this rodeo. What's yores?"

The boy hesitated a moment. "Name's Lee," he said.

"First or last?" the cowboy asked.

"First. My full name's Lee Oliver Rawls." He winced at giving out his name, but if he lied and the guy asked for his ID, he'd be trapped for sure.

"What do yuh do, Lee?"

"Do, whadya mean?"

"Like what's yore event? Bull ridin', saddle broncs, bareback broncs, bulldoggin', ropin', or what?"

"Oh, bull riding."

"Hey, that's my event too, though Pa wants me to get into saddle bronc ridin'. Claims the bulls are too hard on teeth. What bull did yuh draw?"

"What bull did I draw?"

"Yeah, I drawed old Number Eleven, myself. Win a day money on 'im once over to Goldendale, Washington."

"Eleven? I got Twelve. Yes sir, old Number Twelve." Sweat beaded on the boy's lip. He hoped there was a Number Twelve.

"Jeeze! No foolin'! No wonder yuh seem worried. He ain't been rode but once this season. 'Course, most cowboys turn him back. Ever since he killed those two cowboys at Madison Square. Funny how it happened. Hooked one rider one day; trampled another the next. But yuh ever qualify on 'im, man, yore in the money fer shore."

For the first time, Jimmy seemed to take in Lee's ill-fitting clothes.

"Where's yore bull riggin' at, Lee?"

"Lost it. Somebody stole it outa my pickup truck. Clothes too. Had to borrow these from a buddy."

"That buddy of yores must be a big man. Well, yuh can use my riggin'. We'll move yuh up first; I don't ride till the second section."

"Thanks," the boy said.

"That's what friends are fer."

Lee glanced about, looking for a way out of his predicament. Maybe he ought to level with this Jimmy guy and ask his help. But what if the boy told his dad and got him kicked out? Right into the hands of those locals, who were still probably watching every move he made. Best play the game for a few more minutes and watch for an out.

He saw two of his enemies walking the race track. One found a hole underneath the chain-link fence and squirreled through, and the other followed. At that distance they didn't seem to know which one he was, but Lee wheeled and started for the chutes to get out of their line of vision, and to shake Jimmy. But his new friend stuck to him like a bur.

"Wonder who those guys are," Jimmy mused, glancing over at the strangers.

Lee almost confessed, but he held back and the moment was gone.

"Lee," Jimmy said. "Yuh got anybody helpin' yuh get screwed down on yore bull?"

"Helping me? Nope."

"Well, yuh hev now. I know thet old ox pretty good. Yuh want tuh git down on 'im fast, an' don't set there forever. Soon as I jerk the slack outa yore bull rope, take yore wraps around yore glove an' git the hell out on 'im. I'll make sure the clown turns 'im back toward the chute; he'll buck harder in a spin. Once the whistle blows, yuh turn loose o' thet critter'n scramble fer the fence, hear? Ol' Twelve likes tuh knock a feller down an' step on 'is breakfast."

Lee's stomach tightened into knots, and his knees turned to water.

"Oh, an' Lee," Jimmy said, taking a slip of paper from his wallet. "Anybody draws old Number Twelve, we like 'em tuh write down their next o' kin."

13

Jimmy's father trotted by on his spotted horse. "Jimmy," he snapped. "Only three more doggers. Git them bulls in the chutes, hear?"

"Yeah, Dad," the young cowboy replied. "Give me a hand, huh, Lee?"

Lee glanced at the pen of huge gray and black brahmas, then over his shoulder. The two hoods were only a hundred feet away, and yet another had gained the compound and was moving in on him from the side, drawing a net tight about him. He would be safer with the bulls. He followed Jimmy over the fence into the pen.

The big bulls raised their massive horns and shook them angrily at the intruders, the huge humps on their shoulders flopping with the effort.

"Watch thet big black, Lee. Thet's yore bull. He could suck a grape outa a Coke bottle with those horns."

Jimmy yelled and cracked his stock whip in the air. "Haah! Git inta thet chute!" The wise old bulls had done this many a time before and turned into the long corridor leading to the bucking chutes.

"Heads up, boys. Bull's a-comin'. Gate 'em, will yuh, somebody?"

Used to the routine, the bulls moved along through the chutes, and as each bull moved up into place, a cowboy in the arena shoved a cross panel in behind him.

"Yipes," Lee thought. "How do I get out of this mess?" He wished that Jimmy weren't so darn helpful. What he really needed was a handful of these cowboys to rally to his side and drive his attackers away. Fat chance. They'd think he was one of them.

He glanced across the arena, looking for a place to go if he bolted now and ran. His stolen boots were too tight and had already made raw spots the size of silver dollars along his ankle bones. He wished he'd kept his sneakers. This whole bright idea of disguising himself as a cowboy had turned sour. He located the enemy. Three behind the chutes. The two others were lounging across the way, one at each corner of the grandstand.

Climbing up the chute, Jimmy dropped a bull rope of woven hemp down the far side of Number Twelve.

Suspended from the rope, a bell clanked ominously beneath the bull, and the stout black blew a wad of mucous from his nostrils and rattled his horns against the planks. Jimmy settled the rope behind the big hump, while a cowboy on the ground in the arena fished through the slats with a wire and pulled the dangling rope under the bull's belly and up his side. Jimmy caught the end, pushed it through a loop, and pulled it up snug. The bull kicked his belly and set the bell to clanging.

Lee swallowed hard. His throat felt filled with sour cotton.

"Better git ready, cowboy," Jimmy warned as he dropped a flank strap in front of the bull's hips, caught the end and pulled it snug.

Lee was silent; he was afraid his voice wouldn't work, for if it did, it could only betray his fear. He decided to run for it and take his chances, but as he tried to slip off his boots, they seemed glued to his hot, sweaty feet.

Just outside the arena gate, he saw the big red cross on the waiting ambulance. The ambulance! Hey, that was it! He'd go through the motions of coming out on that bull, fall off right out of the chute, pretend to be hurt, and let them cart him off on a stretcher. On the way to the hospital, when

15

the ambulance stopped in traffic, he'd jump up and make his getaway. The bull rattled his horns and a big yellow splinter popped off the chute gate.

"I must be dreaming," Lee thought. "This ain't really happening!"

The three thugs were close. One of them in a ragged T shirt grinned at him as though to say, "We've got you cornered now." If he didn't get out of here fast they might pull him down behind the chutes and, screened from the audience, stomp him out and scatter before anyone could make a move to help.

Limber-legged, he climbed the chute, slipped on the rosined glove Jimmy handed him, and settled down on the bull's back; he let the cowboy pull the rope tight across his hand and double it back, taking a couple of wraps for good measure, and passing the end out between his little and the third finger. He could feel the steaming heat of the bull through his pant leg. He touched the bull with his free hand and was amazed at how soft and sleek it felt.

"Pettin' 'im won't help," Jimmy chided.

Lee stole a glance at the three men. They hung back confused, as though they hadn't expected him to go this far.

Jimmy stepped back down to the ground and grabbed the gate pin.

"Hey, Jimmy!" the announcer called down from the platform above the chutes. "Who's the cowboy? Don't recognise him, and we don't have that Number Twelve bull on the program. What's going on down there anyway?"

Jimmy broke into a sudden grin as he pulled the pin on the gate. "Just a cowboy's way of takin' care of a thief, Mel!" he called up to the announcer.

16

Lee had been taken in by Jimmy's apparent helpfulness. Now, in that instant, he knew the young cowboy had seen him slip into that trailer and help himself, and pegged him for the thief he was. He tried to pull his hand from the rigging and leap for the chute gate, but his hand stuck. The gate swung open and the big bull took a wild, wrenching leap out into the arena.

He tried to lean back, but the bull sucked him forward; the great black horns, ivory tipped, swung back in an arc, smacking Lee's neck. Sharp pains shot through his shoulder, as though his arm was being dragged from the socket. Ahead of him he saw the clown rushing forward, and the bull turned back into a spin. He wanted desperately to get off, but his hand seemed cemented to the rigging.

"Hey, Jimmy!" a cowboy shouted from up on the chutes. "Be damned ef thet guy ain't a-wearin' my Sunday best shirt! It's custom made; hell, there ain't another like it in the country!"

"An' he's got his spurs on upside down!" another answered. "Hey, now, he's really somethin'!"

"Hang in there, Thief!" Jimmy shouted, slapping his chaps as he laughed.

One more wild leap of the bull, and Lee's hand came out of the glove, and he slipped down into the vortex of the bull's spin. Instantly the clown rushed in, slapped Number Twelve in the face, and took the charge, scampering and dodging just one step ahead of those reaching horns, until the bull veered away and, head high, took off for the catch pens at the other end of the arena.

"You all right, Thief?" Jimmy called, kneeling beside the crumpled figure.

17

Lee opened his eyes, spit dirt from his mouth, then closed them again. His throat hurt like hell and his voice just wouldn't come.

"Hey, Frankie! Ain't those yore boots this guy's got on?"

"Look what he's gone and done to my shirt. Tore it all to hell!"

There was a bright welt of blood across Lee's neck where the bull had struck him; his stolen hat lay crumpled beside him, half full of dirt. The fancy shirt was torn from one shoulder, and one spur pointed forward instead of back.

"Better get the ambulance," someone suggested.

"Ambulance, my foot," Jimmy snorted. "He's nothin' but a thief. He's fakin' it! Drag 'im outa here, men!"

Once the cowboys had skidded him out of the arena, they proceeded to take back what was theirs, leaving him clad only in his overalls.

"Saw 'im go inta yore trailer, Harry. Figured 'im fer a thief. Didn't want 'im tuh spook an' run, so I kep 'im busy. Boy did I keep 'im busy. Ef I ain't mistaken, boys, there's three more of his gang behind the chutes."

"Were," a cowboy corrected. "That must be them now, scootin' under the fence out by the backside of the track. Looket them suckers run!"

"Sorry we don't have that rider's name," the announcer was saying to the crowd. "There's been some sort of mix-up on the program. All that cowboy gets, folks, is your applause."

Lee heard scattered clapping. His head and neck hurt, and when he tried opening his eyes, he saw double. Two Jimmys when one would have been plenty. He wanted to explain to Jimmy that those punks were locals, after him to stomp him out because he was a stray, but the words wouldn't come out.

"Yuh get up and get out of here now, Lee Oliver Rawls,

Lee O. Rawls, Lee Overalls, whatever yore name is. We catch yuh aroun' a King Richards rodeo again an' we'll beat yuh up worse than that ol' bull."

"Bull riders to the chutes," the announcer called. When the boy opened his eyes again, Jimmy was gone.

chapter three

⚓

aroncita Madronay made her last run down the track in front of the grandstand, standing upright on two bareback palomino horses, her blonde hair flying as she galloped the horses tandem at breakneck speed and leaped them over a barrier of fire. Maroncita was physically so spectacular she could have drawn the same thunderous applause without the flashy horses, the glittering suit of lights, or the flaming cross rail, just by riding by. As the crowd roared, she flashed them a white-toothed smile, then let her horses gallop up the track a bit before bringing them gradually back under control.

Right now her smile was only skin deep. On the road to Prairie City, she'd blown a tire on her luxurious van and had to change it herself; at the last rodeo, her prop-man-chore-boy had gotten drunk and quit, so now, until she found someone else, she had to torch the jump herself and struggle with her own heavy props. And that idiot, King Richards, had scheduled her too late on the program, after the bull riding, when the sun had dropped behind the grandstand, and the splended sequins on her Rodeo Ben outfit had failed to show to their full glory.

Pulling her horses to a stop as she came back across the arena to the chutes, she slipped down on the back of the off horse, catching the force of the drop with her knees.

Grinning up at her, Ruff Burleigh stepped out from the chutes and moved to take her horses by the reins.

"Keep your hands off my horses, Ruff," Maroncita snapped. "When I need your help I'll ask for it!" She dropped lightly to the ground, elbowed the former champion aside, pulled her reins through the rings of her martingales, and led the animals out of the gate beside the chutes.

"You!" she ordered Lee as he lay outstretched on the ground beyond the gate. "Get out of my way, stupid! I've got to get my horses through."

The figure did not move. She took him for a drunk and hit him a stinging slap across the arm with her reins. Impatient to be on, one of her horses rooted her with its nose, then both horses stepped carefully over the boy's body. As she turned back to close the gate, she saw his face and the blood drying upon his neck and cheek.

"Hey!" she said, kneeling beside him. "You're that first bull rider, aren't you? You hurt bad?"

She cupped her hand gently under his chin and turned his face toward her to inspect the wound.

"Well, I'm damned," she said. "He's just a baby. This is sure some rodeo outfit that doesn't even take care of its wounded."

"You! Jimmy Richards!" she snapped at the young cowboy as he came out of the arena. "You and Ruff pick this kid up carefully and carry him to my van. If he needs a doctor, I'm going to call one and charge it to your dad!"

"He ain't one of ourn," Jimmy protested. "He's a thief. Deserved every bit he got. S'a wonder the cowboys he stole from didn't kill 'im."

"I don't happen to give a damn what he is," Maroncita said, her voice crisp with anger. "He's just a kid, and he's in shock. You and Ruff do as I say, or I'll never work another King Richards rodeo!"

Ruff Burleigh was trying to slip out of the range of her lashing tongue, but at the last moment, for reasons of his own, he turned back and picked the prostrate youth up by his arms, while Jimmy took his feet.

"You lay him right in there on my bed! Never mind the spread. It'll come clean in the wash. I've got to put my horses up, then I'll tend to him."

She slipped the bridles off quickly and replaced them with halters. Hanging the circingles on a hook in her tack room and the blankets upside down on the racetrack rail to dry, she brushed each horse down, then led them in a short circle around the van a few times to cool their backs. "Poor dears," she murmured. "I'll give you a longer walk later. Right now there's someone needs my care more than you."

chapter four

⬦

When Lee regained consciousness, he had no idea where
he was. He seemed to be lying on a cloud of satin, the
air heady with the scent of flowers. The bed kept swaying,
and there was the hum of tires on asphalt. He was traveling
somewhere. Maybe this was a hearse, and he was headed to
his own funeral! He tried to call out for help, to let them
know that he was still alive, but he couldn't make a sound.
He sagged back on the pillows, his head pounding with dull
pain. He had never dreamed such luxury existed. Maybe this
was Heaven; no, it couldn't be Heaven. His mom had told
him that in Heaven there wasn't any such thing as pain.

When he awoke again, he saw that instead of a hearse, he
was lying on an elegant bed, in a luxuriously appointed and
feminine trailer, headed for parts unknown. He was alone,
surrounded by temptation. There were paintings on the wall.
Real paintings, not prints. His stepfather, Slick, had taught

him the difference when he taught him to steal. He'd come in from a motel job with a whole stack of pictures he thought might be worth some dough. Slick took one look at them and flew into a rage, knocking him against the wall of the abandoned store they used as a safe house. "Nothin' but cheap!" he shouted. "Cheap! Cheap! Teach you to drag in somethin' we can't sell!"

Along the wall was a curved-front glass case, glittering with silver bits and spurs, a porcelain bowl edged with a pale green stripe with a spray of painted pink roses below, a gleaming white pitcher and basin, and on a lower shelf, bronze figures depicting every event in rodeo. Everything held securely in place against sudden stops. That stuff had to be class!

From the sounds of traffic, they had to be coming to a fair-sized city. He resolved to get up, put on his clothes, find a blanket or suitcase in which to hide his loot; then, when the van stopped for a red light, he'd step into the wind, take off without the driver, whoever it was, even knowing he was gone. If he couldn't peddle the stuff locally, he'd make a collect call to one of Slick's old contacts, who might tell him how to cash in.

He nestled down, allowing himself one last moment to enjoy the softness of the bed. "Slick." He grinned. "What a wipe out!" His stepfather had sold some stuff to the wrong customer, and by now, he must be awaiting trial. In a way, he was glad his mom was dead and would be spared knowing that her old man was running a network of kids he'd taught everything from purse snatching to heavier stuff.

When the cops had stormed the safe house and picked up Slick, he and Eddy Santos had hidden in the rafters of an adjacent warehouse until the heat was off. Then the two of them had hitchhiked, doing a lot of walking and darn little riding, until a trucker had come along with only one seat. They flipped, and he won. He split the eight dollars in his pocket with Eddy and rode the truck over the Sierras through Nevada clean up into Montana. He hoped Eddy was all right. He'd talked of going to a sister somewhere in Nevada, that is, if Immigration hadn't picked her up already and bundled her back to Mexico.

Gritting his teeth with pain, he forced himself up from the bed. In a closet he found a suitcase perfect for loot. Not too fancy for a working stiff. But he couldn't find his clothes. The closets were full of women's stuff he couldn't wear. Here he was, naked as a jaybird, and nothing except a bunch of women's fancy riding outfits!

So that was it! This van belonged to that woman trick rider, and she was on her way to another rodeo somewhere. From behind him, he heard a horse nicker. This had to be one of those big, long horse vans with built-in living quarters. What a palace! She must do all right for herself.

But where the hell were his clothes? Without trousers, he might as well be in prison here. He started to get angry, pacing the floor of the long, narrow van like an animal in a zoo cage. All that stuff here to steal and no way to get away with it!

His head throbbed, and he felt chilled. As he used the bathroom, he looked in the mirror and got a shock. His face was a mess. Hair standing up like on the back of a scared cat. Lower lip puffed like Eddy's, the time he stole the trombone.

Staggering back to the big bed, he fell into it and pulled

25

up the covers. His head swam dizzily, and when he opened his eyes, there were two of everything again. Two matching chairs, two faces on the picture of the young cowboy on the dresser. He closed his eyes against reality; the swaying motion of the van lulled him to sleep.

chapter five

He awoke to feel the vehicle lurching over rough ground. In the distance he heard the sound of cattle bawling and figured they had pulled into another rodeo grounds somewhere. He lay in the big bed, enjoying his aloneness, though he was starting to get hungry. The van stopped, backed up, then stopped again. He heard the click of a heavy latch, the creaking of hinges; the stomping of horses' hooves sent vibrations through the van, and it shifted levels a bit as someone unloaded a cargo of horses from behind the rear panel. The gate slammed shut with a clang.

He touched his face gingerly. The lip still felt as though he'd been stung by a hornet, and his jaw creaked. If he managed to get any food, he wondered if he could chew.

The door to the living quarters clicked open, and the woman entered, carrying a package done up in brown paper. He pulled the blankets up tight against his chest.

"Well," she said brightly. "I see my patient is awake at last!"

He tried to talk but couldn't make the words come. Instead he glared at her angrily and pointed to his bare chest.

She laughed. "Oh, your clothes. I took them to a laundromat, but they were so dirty that when soap and water hit them, they disintegrated."

She tossed the package on the bed beside him. "Here! I bought you a whole new outfit. Nothing comes for free around here, though. You can work them off. I need someone with a few muscles to take care of my horses and manage the props for my acts."

Where was his voice? He wanted to tell her he was going to get her for kidnapping, carrying him away from Prairie City without his consent. He glared at her, but all he could do was gurgle.

Maroncita Madronay smiled at him as though she read his thoughts. "You can call the police if you want. My guess is you've got a record as long as a reata, and you aren't about to get the police involved."

It was a direct hit, and the boy flushed.

She tossed his wallet on the bed. "I already looked at your ID," she said, sitting down beside him, laying her hand on his forehead. "Tell me, Lee Oliver Rawls. How do you feel?"

Shaking with an anger he couldn't explain, the boy scuttled back from her touch.

Cita Madronay shrugged, got up, went to the refrigerator, and began the process of cooking up a meal of soup and sandwiches.

"I expect you're starved," she said. "You won't remember it because you weren't being very good company at the time, but I had a doctor over before we left Prairie. Said you had a concussion and had best sleep it off. I couldn't just dump you out on the ground, could I? He also said for you to leave off heavy foods for a day or two. So how about a little soup?"

The boy lay silent, pretending to be asleep.

Maroncita shrugged. "Well, look, son. That mad you've got is riding on your back, not mine. I'll go feed my horses while you get dressed. Soup's on the stove. You want to lay there and let it get cold, you lay there; you want to come out and help me feed, then you come do it. You want to go down the road, you go down the road. The clothes are yours to keep. No good-byes. You don't owe me a thing."

She laid out a bath towel across a chair. "There's a shower in that compartment, and plenty of soap and hot water. I suggest you use all three of them. Your face is a fright!" Leaving him on his own, she went out the door, closing it behind her.

For some minutes he lay quiet, ignoring the package, trying to figure out what to do. It was scary not being able to talk. He didn't know how to get along.

He glanced at the package, let it rest for a few moments; then curiosity got the better of him. He reached out one bare arm and poked a finger through the wrapping paper, teasing out a window. Hey, she hadn't been kidding him! He stripped the paper off eagerly. Two new shirts, two pairs of Wranglers. Must be a dozen pairs of socks. Underwear. A brown belt with a big brass buckle. And real cowboy boots! All that must have cost her a bundle. And "no strings," she'd said. He couldn't believe how dumb she was. Well, he'd just put on what clothes he could wear, pack the rest of them in a bundle, and leave!

He rolled out of bed, grabbed the towel off the chair and took a hot shower, gingerly soaping the wounds on his face

29

and neck. Putting on the new finery, he paraded in front of the mirror, then took a look out one of the side windows. There she was out on the track, riding one horse, leading three. He could make his getaway without her seeing him go.

He looked longingly at the silver and bronze in the glass case. He hated to leave all that stuff; but if she came back and found it missing, she'd have the cops on his tail. No way could he get by with stealing it now. He stuffed his spare clothing in the extra shirt and bundled it up, tying it with the sleeves. Gulping down a bowl of soup, he left the dish in the sink, then, carrying his bundle, he stepped out into the world.

Across the way, Jimmy Richards and his father were unloading roping steers from a big aluminum cattle truck.

Jimmy glanced over at him and straightened up. "Hey, Thief!" he called. "Look at them shiny new clothes! Whatcha got in thet bundle? Maroncita's silver?"

Lee slowed down and then stopped. Slowly he turned toward the van. Taking up a manure fork, he set his bundle in a manger and began cleaning out the stalls. He was tired of running. Right now, come to think about it, this chance was as good as any other. He'd stick around awhile and work until he had a few bucks in his jeans.

chapter six

Maroncita returned from exercising her horses to find a huge pile of straw bedding behind the horse stalls of the van; but the inside was spotless. Instead of cleaning the areas where the straw was damp, that fool boy had cleaned them all. For an instant her lips thinned with vexation, then she smiled. The kid stood tall and straight, looking off across country as if watching something, ignoring her, yet obviously painfully aware of her presence. He was taller than she had imagined. She guessed he was about seventeen. Somehow he was like a puppy, afraid to be beaten, yet so desperately needing approval.

"I can't believe it," she said. "You've done such a good job. Look at that horse section; it's factory clean." She didn't add that she'd just cleaned it a few hours before.

She handed him the ropes to three of her horses, keeping a white mare for herself. "Help me tie them up," she said.

"Watch out for this one, though. She'll kick and bite at strangers. Won't let anybody touch her but me, so stay plumb out of her way."

The boy took the ropes and followed sullenly, keeping at a distance, his gaze on the ground.

"Let me show you how to tie them properly, Lee, so they don't step over their ropes and get tangled. Be especially careful of the palomino on the right. That's Blondie. She likes to untie knots, and when she gets loose, she tends to go visiting."

Blondie rubbed her nose on the boy's sleeve, and he drew it away quickly.

For half an hour Maroncita stood patiently, teaching the boy how to tie a bolen and the other knots she insisted that he use, making him tie them and untie them until he had them memorized. "There's a good reason for tying them up this way," she explained. "Even if they spook and pull back against the rope, the animals won't choke, and you can still untie them quickly in an emergency."

She picked up a brush and showed him how to groom the horses properly, until their coats gleamed like satin. She tied the white mare apart, so that he could move freely about the others without fear of getting kicked. The mare kept turning her head to look at the stranger.

"I hate breaking in a new man," Maroncita said, "because it's often weeks before she really settles down. If she's still nervous tomorrow, I'll use Tune as part of my tandem fire jump team rather than take a chance at getting hurt."

The boy brushed the horses carefully, methodically, but he was sullen. It began to wear on her nerves. Since she had first seen him, he hadn't said one word. She didn't need that. She'd let him stick around until she finished her contract performances at Great Falls; then, when she pulled out for the next show, she'd leave him behind.

The mean mare, Jezebel, kept watching the boy as though waiting for a chance to kick him if he came too close; but as he took off with the wheelbarrow to get a couple of bales of fresh bedding straw, the mare suddenly began nickering to him as though he were her lost foal. Leaning back against her tie-rope, she busted it, then whirled and thundered after him.

Maroncita rushed to intercept her, but the animal swept on by and, mane flying, charged after the boy.

"Get over the fence," she screamed. "Jezebel's loose; she's after you!"

The boy looked at the fence, then at the onrushing mare. There was no time to run.

Maroncita looked around wildly for help, but there was no one near. When next she sought out the boy, the mare had skidded to a stop and was holding her nose out meekly to be scratched. Timidly, he put out his hand and laid it on her neck. When he turned and walked back to the other horses, she followed along behind.

Maroncita didn't quite know what to say, so she matched the boy's silence with her own. She replaced the broken cotton rope with one of nylon, while the boy brushed Jezebel down. When he left again to get the bedding, the mare watched him go and nickered, but made no attempt on the rope. It was as though she had established contact with him, and for the moment, that was enough.

Later that morning, Maroncita showed Lee how to set up the hurdle for the jump of fire, how to saturate the padded rail with flammable liquid and set it afire without getting singed himself. For every time she made the jump before an audience, she might do it half a dozen times in practice, striving for perfection, getting her horses used to the arena. He didn't get in the way like most kids, and during her performances that afternoon, he was watchful and alert, ever ready to jump in and make himself useful.

Somehow, her resolve to leave him behind at Great Falls faded, and she took him along. He sat in the cab of the van, with a map of Montana spread over his knees, and navigated for her. One moment the town where she had contracted to perform next was only a name on a map to him; the next, as they swept over a rise or around a bend in the highway, it became a reality.

After a week, Lee could have taken that jump down and put it back up in his sleep. The horses seemed to love him, and Maroncita had only to station Lee a few yards down the track from the hurdle, and the galloping, plunging team raced directly to him, slowing down and stopping without her having to pull hard on their mouths.

He had been with her almost ten days when, as she sat in the shade outside the rodeo office, waiting to pick up her paycheck, she watched him from afar, taking Jezebel to water. He reached over the mare's ears to crush a horsefly on her forehead, then stroked her neck with affection.

He was totally unlike any boy she had ever known. A watcher, not a talker. He had never spoken. She wondered if he had a voice at all, and if he had, what it would sound like. When he wasn't busy, he watched everything that went on around the rodeo, and when she practiced, he sat quietly by, inconspicuous, part of the shadows along the fence, yet jumping up unbidden to change saddles for her, bring up her next mount, or groom her sweaty horses.

She'd put together a bedroll for him of canvas and some

extra blankets, and when darkness marked the end of a long day, he would lay out his bed among the mares, as though they had a silent agreement to protect each other against harm. During the long nights, she would hear through her open window his gentle, even breathing, and the contented snufflings of the animals as they nosed about the hay in their mangers.

Sometimes as she lay, she wondered about his past. There was a nervous tension about him, as though he feared that any moment someone out of yesterday would come marching around the corner. Seventeen-years-old going on a hundred. He had good features, but the burdens of growing up had etched themselves into his face.

For a time during the first days, she had tried to trap him into a conversation. Then she had just accepted his silence quietly, impersonally. She even came to wish some of the others around her who had nothing to say wouldn't insist on saying it.

One afternoon, after he had been around for two weeks or more, Bum, an Australian shepherd cowdog belonging to Jimmy Richards, came over to Maroncita's van and set up residence in the cool beneath it. The boy didn't seem to notice Bum's adoring glances, but when dusk came, and a light summer rain came in off the mountains, Lee moved his bedroll into the tack room for the night, and the dog followed along and lay outside, guarding him as he slept.

In the morning, Jimmy came over to get his dog, but when he tried to put a leash on Bum, the dog bit him on the hand.

chapter
seven

✣

ee had never been around animals before, and why
they seemed to cotton to him, he had no idea. He only
knew he felt sort of happy and relaxed when he got near
them. He hadn't planned to stay, but they held him with
Maroncita. You could trust an animal in ways you
couldn't trust people. He liked the woman's mares especially
—Blondie, Jezebel, Tune, and Breeze. Liked to curry them
until they gleamed. Liked to oil their hooves and polish them
to a high luster. Liked to watch them run straight and fast,
manes and tails flying, when she did her trick riding act. The
faster they leveled out and ran, the smoother they seemed to
glide.

He couldn't get over the things she could do ahorseback.
She even had one act where she went down one side of a
galloping horse, swung underneath, and came up the other

side of the horse into the saddle. Sometimes he could hear the flying hooves strike her body as they came forward.

There was nothing fake about her acts; they were dangerous. During one early one morning practice, as she rode by the empty stands at a mad gallop, standing on the saddle, leaning forward, no hands, wind sculpting her body like the figurehead of a ship and straightening her long blonde hair out behind her like a ghost trying to catch up, her mare stumbled a little and she went down.

He thought she would never stop rolling. He was about to rush out there to see if she was killed, when she got back up, brushed herself off, caught up her mare, checked her for loose shoes, and darned if she didn't go through that same ride again, this time even faster. As she thundered by him, he could see that she had a cut on her cheek and blood soaking through her nice blouse, but she never quit practicing. She was one gutsy lady!

That very morning, they had set up the fire jump, and when she had done her practice tandem jumps, they had wired the apparatus against the grandstand along the track where it would be out of the way until time for the performance. When one of the mares spooked at the empty grandstand, she made him lead the animal back and forth past the stands one hundred times to show her there was nothing to be afraid of.

Later that morning, once she had gone back to her trailer to clean up and take care of her cut, he slipped up on the mare's back and rode her instead of leading her. He felt just like part of the horse, as though maybe he'd been a famous horseman in another life. The mare kept glancing back at him, as though she enjoyed having him there and wanted to do what would please him best. It pleased him to ride, and he was surprised at how much technique he had picked up just watching, day after day.

He rode until he started geting sore, then slipped off, untied the other horses, and threw the lead ropes over the necks of his charges. He walked back through the crowd of cowboys and their horses, and his mares followed along, noses to his elbows. Each one of them he tied up securely and fed them wafers of bright green hay.

At noon time, Maroncita gave him money to buy some lunch over at the concession stand, since she wasn't feeling well, and told him to be back at one sharp to help her get ready for her act. She'd put some powder on her face to hide the purple bruise forming around the cut on her cheek, and it didn't look so bad.

He bought a Pepsi and two hamburgers, then sat on the fence and watched the cowboys limber up their mounts. Some of the cowboys he remembered from as far back as the Prairie City Rodeo. King Richards and Jimmy, of course. Ruff Burleigh, and quite a few others whose names he didn't know. Everyone ignored him. These contestants took notice of rodeo people and pretty girls. Everyone else was invisible.

The rodeo clown at this rodeo site was a different breed of man. He was a tall, gangly, moon-faced, easy-going cowboy named Slim Pickens, with a pinto mule named Judy, and a big blue horse somebody next to Lee told him was an appaloosa. The horse had white spots all over his rump, and Slim called him Dear John. Must have been a dozen rodeo kids followed behind Slim everywhere he went, and once Lee had seen him buy ice cream over at the stands for every kid around. It was "Hey, Slim" this and "Hey, Slim" that. One question after another, but the big guy took the time to answer them all.

Slim even said "hello" to him, but he turned away as though he hadn't heard. He'd made up his mind his voice would never come back and he would just make silence part of his thing.

He thought about how nice it would be to be invisible, so he could just drift around watching people, and they would accept him, kind of because they wouldn't know he was there. He could eat at restaurants even, without having to pay. All his life he'd had to keep one eye peeled for trouble, and now there wasn't much that escaped him. He'd left those Prairie City goons behind, but if he strayed from the contestants' area at any other place, there might be locals just as bad. Maroncita had gotten him a button with a ribbon identifying him as arena help, and he wore it like a sheriff's star.

He missed his friend, Eddy Santos. In his mind he started a letter to Eddy. Dear Eddy. Dear? Kind of stupid the way people were supposed to begin letters. Friend Eddy. He liked that better. You'd never guess where I am or the things that have been happening to me. I mean, what would you think if you knew your friend, Lee, had come out of a rodeo chute on a brahma bull, gotten a concussion, and ended up traveling around Montana working for a beautiful lady trick rider, helping her with her act? You'd think that's just a big windy on my part. Nope. It's true. There's a guy here named Jimmy Richards, thinks he's pretty smart. His father is the big honcho puts on these rodeos. Jimmy thinks I'm a thief. Ha! Ha!

Lee finished the last of his lunch and moved back to the van. Jimmy and his father were there talking to Maroncita, and he sensed that their business was far from social. Lee

39

pitched in, flaking out some hay to Maroncita's horses to show that he was gainfully employed. He couldn't follow their conversation, but guessed they were complaining about his presence around the rodeo.

When they had left, Maroncita called him over. "Well, Lee. Can you guess what that was all about? For some reason, Jimmy still thinks that you are—well—dishonest. They are a little bit hostile about your hanging around here. I depend for my livelihood on contracts to perform at various rodeos around the country. There are other trick riders to be had, like Jeannie Godshall or Bernadette Cabral, and I can't risk making King Richards mad.

"Now you might be dishonest and you might not be. But I took a chance on you, and I'll stick by you. You've got a good way with horses that, whether you know it or not, is pretty unusual. So I told them to go to hell. You were staying. But I'd take it as a personal favor if you'd keep your nose clean. You understand, friend?"

Lee nodded, turning away lest she see his face. He was already composing a letter to his friend Eddy Santos.

Friend Eddy. You'll never believe what just happened. That woman I work for went to bat for me!

chapter eight

Lee was exercising Maroncita's mares on the track, the day before his sixth rodeo was to begin, riding one and leading the others, when a big semi truck with Alberta license plates drove in off the highway, and the driver asked Lee where he could find King Richards.

"Got a load of green horses out of Alberta for him to try out as bucking stock. That is, if he's interested."

The boy pointed over to the stock pens behind the chutes, where Jimmy and his father were working cattle. The driver left his big diesel engine idling, ambled over and climbed the corral fence, waiting until King found a stopping point and came over to the fence to talk. His curiosity whetted, Lee rode his horse close enough to hear.

"I was headed south with a load of horses," the driver explained. "Thought maybe I could interest you in trying them out for buckers. They're all young horses, mountain raised, and big enough to be saddle broncs. You interested in look-ing?"

King nodded. "Always on the lookout fer new blood," he said. "But we'd have tuh try 'em out."

"Of course," the driver said. "Where do you want me to unload?"

The big man pointed to the unloading chute. "Over there. We're 'bout done here, and we'll be over tuh clear that pen with the water trough in it. And yuh help yuhself tuh some hay."

He signaled a cowboy on a pinto horse to turn the cattle out the gate into the feeding area in the center of the race-track, then turned to his son, Jimmy. "Think we can round up enough warm bodies this morning to give 'em a try?" he asked.

Jimmy nodded. "Always cowboys around who could use a few bucks. I'll go see what I can come up with while you and the driver unload." He spotted Lee, and his eyes lit up.

Lee had dropped from the back of his mare and was examining her hoof for a stone, when Jimmy ambled up.

"Say, Thief," he said. "Howja like to learn how to ride saddle broncs? My dad's got a truckload of green broncs to try out. He'll pay five bucks a head and furnish the riggin'. Be a good chance tuh practice another event beside bulls. Yuh want in?"

Lee shook his head, set down the hoof, and began buffing an imaginary scratch on the saddle with his sleeve, rubbing it to a hot polish.

"Well, OK," Jimmy said. "Ef yore scared, reckon I can find all sorts of cowboys'd like to make some easy money. Hell, maybe there won't be a bucker in the lot. Well, yuh change yore mind, mosey over there to the chutes."

Lee took the horses back to the van, then saddle soaped one of Maroncita's saddles and carried it back to the tack room. He bet that rigging hadn't looked that pretty since it was new. He tried to tune Jimmy Richards out of his mind, but he kept hearing him. Scared? Well if he was scared a little bit, it was because he'd never done that sort of thing. And what if he came out on a saddle bronc right in front of Maroncita and fell on his head the very first jump? He looked around for her, then vaguely remembered that she was off to town with Slim Pickens' pretty red-haired wife, Maggi.

Locking the tack room, he drifted over to the chutes.

"Well, Thief, yuh ready to try some?" Jimmy asked.

Lee nodded.

Slim Pickens was helping put the horses into the chutes. He looked different without his clown gear. In the arena he wore any sort of outlandish clothing that would get a laugh, from Indian headdresses of feathers, fur, or buffalo horns, to a matador's hat, but never the baggy pants and grease paint of the circus clown. He counted on his antics and the mobility of his rubbery, small-jawed face, and its occasional prominence of teeth, to add to his arena personality.

Right now he was being handsome, being himself, the big, talented cowboy who could do any event in rodeo, from saddle bronc riding, bareback, and bulls, to bulldogging. He had on a neatly tailored shirt, a clean white Stetson, new Levi's, and sharkskin boots.

"I'd try out summa them suckers fer yew," he apologized to King, "but I promised Maggi and her daughter, Darryl Anne, I'd meet 'em in town."

But Lee couldn't see that he was in any hurry to leave the action.

Jimmy came through the arena gate packing a bronc

43

saddle on his hip and flopped it on the ground in front of Lee. "Set down on it," he commanded, "and I'll adjust the stirrups to fit."

Friend Eddy, Lee thought to himself. You'll never guess what's happening to me right now!

When the stirrups were set, Slim Pickens took the saddle and swung it up on the gate. The big brown horse in the chutes ducked away from the saddle and snorted, peering through the slats of the chute gate at this strange new world. Slim climbed the gate and eased the saddle down onto the animal's back. The horse fired a backwards kick with one hind hoof, testing the materials in the cross gate with a sledge-hammer blow.

"Easy now, fella," Slim said softly. "Nobody's goin' to hurt yew."

Jimmy extended a wire hook under the horse's belly and brought the cinch ring up where Slim could reach it with the latigo; then, as the big cowboy cinched up the saddle, Jimmy drew up the sheepskin-lined flank strap, letting it hang loose, but ready to be pulled snug when the rider was about ready.

Lee put on the pair of dull spurs Jimmy handed him. He'd practiced with a pair of Maroncita's and was careful not to put them on upside down.

Even so, Slim seemed to read his lack of experience. He went to his trailer and came back with his own chaps and buckled them on the boy; then, without anyone even asking, he stationed himself on the catwalk behind the chute, and, as Lee stood poised above the horse, waiting to get down on him, Slim grasped the boy by the belt, ready to jerk him out of the way should the green bronc rear and come over backwards.

With his free hand, Slim reached over the horse's mane

and picked up the heavy braided buck-rein, which ran to the bronc's halter. "Take it about here, Lee," he advised, "about an inch behind the swells. Git it too short, and he'll jerk yew over his head; too long, and yew'll go over the cantle. When he comes out, first jump, turn yore toes out an' catch 'im in the neck with yore spurs. Bronc spurs are dull; they'll tickle 'im, not hurt 'im." He gave Lee a reassuring pat on the shoulder. "Git down on 'im now, with yore right hand reachin' fer the breeze. Yew can ride 'im, cowboy! I know yew can!"

Lee took his rein, measured it off, settled down on the horse, and found the stirrups with his toes. His arches both charley-horsed with nervous tension. He wanted out of there, though, and nodded to Jimmy, who lost no time, pulled the pin, and swung the gate open wide. The bronc stood stock still, ears back, until Slim waved his hat, and the startled animal shifted crablike out the chute, then went galloping along the fence.

Lee remembered suddenly to use his spurs, and the animal ducked his head and went to bucking in earnest, soaring so high Lee thought he would never start down. When the bronc lit, it was with a jolt that snapped Lee's neck and up he soared again.

The hours he'd spent on Maroncita's horses stood him in good stead. "I'm riding him!" Lee thought in astonishment. "Heck, this is easy!"

The next giant leap, however, threw him to one side, and the horse, feeling his weight shift, spun around, and suddenly, he was on the ground. The horse kicked at him, barely missing his head.

King Richards rode on past him without even glancing down to see if he were hurt. *I'm just a body to him*, Lee thought. *A sack of potatoes tied to the saddle would do as well.*

Two riders ran the horse back into the catch pens at the far end of the arena, and moments later, they came back, holding the saddle by the stirrups between them, dropping it by the chutes. Jimmy looked a little disappointed that Lee hadn't been killed.

"Yew did fine, Lee," Slim said with a friendly grin. "Yew managed two or three pretty good jumps on him where yew looked like a real pro. Next time I bet yew'll ride."

The next three horses hardly bucked at all, but galloped like barn-sour plow horses heading home for their grain. But they gave Lee some much-needed confidence. At five dollars a head, run or buck, it seemed like easy money.

The next animal, however, was a big, showy palomino, bright as the sun, with flaxen mane and tail, and a JOE branded on the left hip. The animal looked far too pretty to be in the group.

"Reckon yew better watch this one, cowboy," Slim advised. "He don't seem tew belong in the bunch, and there's got tew be a good reason someone let him go. He's halter broke and even got a saddle mark or two on 'is back. My guess is he's somebody's spoilt saddle horse, an' he's jes' liable tew make yew earn yore five."

The horse was all saddled in the chutes, and Lee had just settled on his back, when Maroncita's voice broke the hush.

"What's going on here?" she demanded. "King Richards, that kid's no cowboy! You turn him out on that bronc and he'll get hurt for sure!"

Lee's heart gave a great leap. Maroncita was on the fence watching, and now that he had a little confidence he figured that for her, he could make one helluva ride.

46

"Don't pull that pin, Jimmy Richards, you hear?"

"Aw, this horse is gentle, Maroncita. He nursed his mother when she was sick," Jimmy said.

Lee went on measuring off his bucking rein, and Slim's big hand tightened on his belt. Behind him another cowboy held the end of the flank strap, ready to tighten it as the horse left the chute.

"Yuh want 'im, kid?" King Richards called, letting Lee decide for himself.

He nodded his head, and Jimmy pulled the pin, then swung the gate wide.

The yellow horse came out of the chute like a misfired rocket, nearly scraping Lee off on the gate. He caught sight of Jimmy's eyes, fear written on his face as the bronc lunged and nearly took his hat off with his teeth. Lee's first impulse was to jump off and let the horse buck on without him; then he remembered Maroncita and felt the urge to go as far as he could with style. He turned his toes out and spurred the way Slim had told him. He was going to ride that horse or die trying.

"Stay with 'im, kid!" Slim shouted above the din, leaping down off the chute and following along, coaching the boy in his excitement. "Lean back! Lean back! Atta boy!"

Four or five wild, fast jumps out, the big horse sucked back and went into a spin. There was a yard of daylight between Lee and the saddle, but he fell back on it, got his stirrups, and miraculously picked up the rhythm. The crafty old bucker straightened again, pitching straight ahead, biting at his boot, then turning on his side in midair to kick at the boy in the saddle.

Making a soaring leap, the horse kicked high, then slammed his front feet into the turf and sucked around sideways as he soared again. Lee went up with him, but lost him in midair and lit cleanly on his feet as the bronc kicked back at him, missed by a yard, and galloped off to stand quietly, his job done, by the catch pens.

"Lookit thet son of a buck." Slim grinned. "Thet ain't thet old palomino's first trip out of a chute, yew can bet on thet." He grabbed Lee by the shoulders and gave him an er-cited shake. "Let me tell yew somethin', Lee. Fer a button, yew shore done OK."

Since the instant he left the chute, Lee had forgotten to breathe. Now he began to stagger, and his chest heaved as he took in air in big gulps. He straightened up, hoping to catch an astonished smile from Maroncita, but instead she gave him a hard, angry look, dropped from the fence, whirled, and stalked back toward her van. Stung, he moved back to the chutes to await his next horse.

He felt the big clown's hand on his shoulder as he walked. "Yessir, Lee, yew're doin' jus' fine," he said. "And now fer the best news. There's only twenty-three more of them suckers left tew ride!"

chapter
nine

By the time Lee had come out of the chute on a dozen horses, he was so weary he could hardly climb the gate for another ride, and some other cowboys had to move in to spell him off. He wondered why Jimmy didn't try a few for practice, but contented himself with pulling the gate pin for whose who did. Of the truckload of horses, King found only six to his liking, one of which was the yellow horse. Many of the rest had bucked hard, but not well enough to satisfy the veteran producer.

"Good saddle broncs," King ventured to the driver as he paid him with a draft, "are like athletes. There are plenty of good ones around, but danged few greats."

That evening after the rodeo, Jimmy came to Maroncita's van with Lee's check. He let the envelope flutter down to the floor of the tack room so Lee would have to pick it up, then left without even thanking him for a hard and dangerous day's work.

When Maroncita finally came out of her van, Lee offered her the check to pay for his clothes. She turned him down with a shake of her head as she walked over toward her horses.

"Look, Lee," she said, breaking her silence at last. "I appreciate the offer, but no thanks. That money came to you hard; I know it did. You keep it and take some girl to a movie." She moved back towards the van. "Better come in and eat," she said. "Supper's getting cold."

As the boy ate, she sat at her dressing table, brushing her long blonde hair, glancing now and then at the reflection of the boy in the mirror. He didn't seem to have much appetite, but then he'd had quite a day. He had good reason to be tired. Still not one word from his lips. Maybe there was something wrong with his throat, but she had her doubts. Sometimes he seemed almost ready to talk, then seemed to change his mind. "Well, he's no cowboy," she mused. "He takes his hat off when he eats."

When Lee had finished, he put his dishes in the sink, smiled his thanks and went out the door. Maroncita came out a few minutes later to check her mares in the dusk and found that they had all been groomed and fed. Lee was in his bedroll beside them, apparently asleep.

Lee heard her footsteps, however, and the soft murmur of her voice as she checked her animals and bid them good night. As he lay in his bedroll, he let his mind wander through all sorts of adventures. In one, Ruff Burleigh, drunk and abusive, was making a pest of himself. "Don't, Ruff!" she protested as Ruff tried to put his arm around her.

Lee stepped in quickly, his two long strides taking him

across the dusty corral. Shoving the big cowboy back with one hand, he steadied him for a moment. "You let her plumb alone, Burleigh," he said. "You hear me? You listenin' good?" And then he hit him hard. Biff! Like that! Right on the jaw. The force of the blow spun Burleigh around like a top, and he fell back into a horse trough, from which he rose sputtering, and staggered away, his lesson learned.

"Oh, Lee! Thank you! Thank you! Maroncita said. "How can I ever repay you?"

Lee stood silent for a moment, looking at her, his legs spread like a gunfighter's, his hands on his hips. "Let me count the ways," he said.

He heard the sound of the van door as she opened it, entered, closed it, and locked it against the night.

Friend Eddy, he mused as he dropped off to sleep, *It's been some kind of day!*

chapter
ten

The rodeo started the next day at noon. Lee spent all morning grooming the horses and getting the equipment not only ready but shining for Maroncita's performance. She rode second in the grand entry.

As Lee sat watching from the sidelines, Cita Madronay loped on easily before a long column of sweating, dancing horses of all sizes, colors, shapes, and degrees of condition, ridden by an equal diversity of riders, many of whom seemed to be riding borrowed and unfamiliar mounts and struggled to clamp themselves into ill-fitting saddles. But perhaps their appearances mattered little, for most eyes were on the woman.

There were a few moments of inattention when the sheriff, a big, round-faced redhead in the lead, carrying the flag of the United States, got into a predicament. His horse spooked at the wind-flung banner, causing the sheriff to cant a little to one side, so that the saddle turned, and the horse bucked the rider off, flag and all. But once the sheriff caught the trembling animal, straightened the saddle, tightened his cinch, shook the dust from the sullied flag, and mounted, all attention returned to Maroncita.

Slim Pickens, mounted on his mule, Judy, brought up the rear. He had borrowed an outfit from a jockey and rode his mule as though ready for a race, knees up under his chin, ridiculously cramped and crowded on a saddle that seemed little larger than a wash cloth. As he passed the grandstand, he thumped Judy into an awkward gallop, laid his cheek against the mule's neck and stuck his posterior in the air in a manner that would have made the town banker smile.

Lee was headed back to the van when Slim Pickens, riding Dear John, the big appaloosa, trotted up beside him. "Hey, Lee," he said, grinning down at the boy. "Yew got a minute? By golly, I gotta proposition fer yew."

Lee stopped beside the horse and occupied himself with looking at the horse's hooves, yet was pleased as punch that the famous rodeo clown had singled him out for attention.

"My barrel man didn't show up, and I need somebody to work the barrel fer me in my act. It's worth fifty bucks a performance. Yew game, Lee?"

Lee had no idea what working the barrel meant, but he nodded his head.

"Shore do appeciate thet!" Slim said. "When Cita's done with her trick ridin', yew lope right on over tew the chutes tew help me. I'll ride over tew her van now tew square it with her."

As the clown trotted off on Dear John to talk to Maroncita, Lee, hugging himself with joy, cut across the arena, walking in a dream. Only vaguely did he hear Mel Lambert, the announcer, call out the first bareback bronc rider. There was a big commotion in Chute One, and a small, black bronc shot out of there, firing hard, kicking up at the sky. Towed along with one hand gripping a thick strap riveted to a circingle, the loose end of the flank strap flapping against the bronc's hips, the rider leaned back, spurring wildly, as though determined to rack up points with the judges.

Lee came out of his daze just in time to see the bronc headed right at him. "Yipes!" he thought and leaped out of the way.

Halfway across the arena, the little horse ducked sideways out from under the contestant and dumped him on his head. The wiry youth bounced once and rolled to his feet, shaking his head and grinning foolishly at his friends back at the chutes, while the crowd gave him a hand for one whale of a try.

"That ride might not have seemed long to you folks over there in the grandstands," Mel Lambert said, laughing, "but believe me, to that cowboy it seemed like a whole year!"

Lee went out the gate beside the chutes and angled toward the van. Slim Pickens had been there and gone. Maroncita met him at the door, eyes flashing her anger.

"Of all the stupid fools!" she exclaimed. "You really had to be behind the door, cowboy, when the brains were passed out! Slim Pickens just told me you'd agreed to be his barrel man. You don't even know what a barrel man does, do you? Well, I'll tell you. He gets out there during the bull riding and lets a bull chase him over to a specially made barrel. If he manages to elude the bull without getting gored, he ducks inside, and the bull catches the barrel with his horns and throws the dang thing maybe thirty feet in the air.

"You know what happened to one of Slim's barrel men? That old Harry Rowell bull, Number Twenty-Nine, the same ox that crippled that good clown Homer Holcomb for life, chased Slim's partner into his barrel and hit it so hard he threw it fifty feet, clear out of the arena. The kid came out of that barrel stammering in Gaelic like his ancestors. He's never been right since."

Her face flushed in her anger, and Lee thought he had never seen her look more beautiful. He went over to her mares and began cleaning out the frogs of their hooves with a curved hoof knife, checking as he did so for loose shoes.

"Go ahead, Lee," she said as she mounted Jezebel and reined her toward the track. "Do what you damn please! It's your life. Why should I care what happens to you?"

Lee smiled to himself. If she didn't care, then why was she so angry?

He took a farrier's hammer and a block of steel and tightened Blondie's shoes, finishing the job just as Maroncita came riding back for her. She rode off on the white animal without further comment, leaving him to groom the tandem team by himself.

He began to worry that she was right. He wished there was someone he could consult about the barrel act. When he finished grooming the team, he went over to the arena, intending to tell Slim that he'd changed his mind. But when he got there, Slim was just heading out across the arena on Dear John. The clown gave him a friendly grin, and the boy couldn't bring himself to go back on his word.

Instead, he stood by the fence and watched Slim perform. Dear John had been trained to buck on cue, and once he was out in the arena, he exploded under Slim, tossing the clown higher and higher into the air, but catching him as he fell. Then when Slim got off to see if there was a pine burr under the saddle, every time he tried to put the saddle back on, Dear John would reach back with his teeth and throw the blanket on the ground, and the whole process would start over.

By the time Slim had finished his act, it was time to help Maroncita, and there was no time to think about anything else. Lee was leading three of Cita's mares along the track toward the grandstand, following behind her as she rode Tune, when they passed a gossip of young ladies, all barrel racers waiting to perform.

"Cita!" a tall, willowy girl called out, trotting a sleek, black, hot-blooded mare toward them. "Cita Madronay! Wait up!" The girl wore a pair of tight jeans, a lavender hat, and a matching western shirt, tailored to fit her slender body. Her hair hung in a long, straight ponytail to the middle of her back.

She flung herself down from her horse, draped the split reins over the low fence, climbed over, and rushed up to Maroncita, who leaned from her saddle to give her a hug.

"Pam!" Maroncita smiled. "It's nice to see you, child. You're out of school for the summer and back to your old love, barrel racing! I'll bet your dad's pleased."

"Oh, you know Dad. I think he'd rather I stayed home on the ranch. I think he's afraid every time I compete that my old mare will knock down all the barrels and embarrass him. I love to win, sure, but some of these girls have a head start on me with a dozen rodeos under their belt buckles already this season. My mare's still packing a winter hay belly that's costing a couple of seconds every run."

Lee's three horses stood waiting beside him, rubbing their

noses on his arm. Tune turned her head toward him and nickered as though making sure he was near.

"This is Lee Oliver Rawls," Maroncita said, nodding at him. "Lee, this is Pam Richards. She's Jimmy's sister, and one whale of a barrel racer. She'll be champion of the world some day, I'm sure."

Lee smiled silently as he glanced at the girl, then lowered his gaze to the ground. He wished Maroncita would move along.

"Next barrel racer, Cyrille Rickbell," Mel Lambert announced. "On deck, Ginny Jayne. Pam Richards get ready."

"Oh my," Pam said. "Got to run. See you all later. Can't wait to catch your act, Cita!"

Maroncita glanced back at Lee, a faint smile of amusement on her face. She might have been thinking to chide him for his shyness, but he was busy stroking the foretop of one of the mares, and she rode forward, leaving him to follow.

There were three barrels placed at intervals, forming a triangle in the arena. As the flag man dropped his flag to start the clock for the final contestant, Pam came flying across the starting line. Ponytail straight out behind in the wind, she leaned forward, urging her animal on. She circled to the right around the first barrel, lined out toward the far barrel on the right, circled it, then streaked for the barrel on the left. Her stirrup bumped the barrel by mistake, and the crowd groaned as the barrel tipped and did a balancing act. There was a mass sigh of relief as the barrel settled back down. Leaning forward, Pam applied her crop, streaking for the finish line as fast as the big, black blood horse could run.

"Eighteen point one seconds for Pam Richards," the announcer said. "Not quite good enough, ladies and gentlemen, for third place. And now, while they're removing the barrels from the arena for the calf roping, may I present that world famous trick rider, none other than the beautiful Maroncita Madronay, doing a fender drag!"

Maroncita went galloping past the grandstand, hanging upside down from the saddle, her long hair almost trailing the ground. On the return run, she executed a perfect shoulder stand, her sandaled toes pointed to the sky.

As she righted herself and slipped down into the saddle, there was a burst of applause at Lee's elbow, and he turned to find Pam Richards standing there beside him. "Isn't she wonderful?" Pam beamed. "There's really no one like her in the whole wide world!"

Lee acknowledged his agreement with a smile but had no time to do more. Stepping away from the fence, he caught up the reins of Maroncita's mount, helped her off, then, locking his fingers together into a stirrup, caught up her foot and helped her spring into the saddle of her next mount.

That afternoon, King Richards put in the new saddle broncs as rerides. If a cowboy drew a saddle bronc that failed to buck in the contest, he was given a replacement. Ruff Burleigh came out of the chute on a big bay horse that for some reason had an off day and galloped off across the arena with his nose stuck in the air, as though looking for a friend in the crowd. When the judges granted him a reride, Ruff drew none other than the big yellow horse Lee had tried out.

Lee felt he had a personal stake in that horse and moved over to the chutes, where he sat shivering with excitement as the big, stout cowboy set his saddle on the horse's back, moved it well up on the withers, cinched it tight, gave instructions to the flank man to pull the flank strap up a notch, and settled down on the animal's back. "Let's have him," he snapped at the gate man.

"Former Champion All-Around Cowboy, Ruff Burleigh, out of Chute Number Two, on a reride named Yellow Fever," the announcer called.

Go, horse, go! Lee thought.

Ruff came out of the chute with an unlit cigarette stuck jauntily between his lips, a Burleigh trademark. As the big palomino bucked past Lee, the boy swore he could see a twinkle of recognition in his tight, little-pig eyes. After the second jump, Ruff, who was leading the other bronc riders for first place, seemed to realize he was in for a storm. With a great crooked leap, Yellow Fever turned on his side and kicked at Ruff's ear, loosening the cowboy in the saddle. When the horse hit the ground, he shifted sideways one jump, then the other direction the next; and each time he fence-railed, Ruff got a little looser in the saddle. As though aware of an advantage, Yellow Fever sucked back, then whirled, heading right back toward the chutes from which he had come. With one wild leap, the big bronc left Ruff hanging upside down in midair, and he hit the ground like a two hundred pound sack of harness.

Lee giggled to himself. It wasn't just that he was pleased by his friend the horse's performance. As the bulky cowboy smashed face-first into the dust, he swallowed his cigarette. He staggered out of the arena holding his stomach tight with both hands; and his face beneath the arena grime was a curious shade of green.

59

chapter eleven

riend Eddy Lee mused as he led Maroncita's tandem team out the gate onto the race track. The guard at the gate recognized him and grinned as he passed through, then moved to close it behind him. *Friend Eddy, you'll never guess the mess I've gotten myself into now. It all started when the clown—whose name is Louis Lindley, but he goes by the name Slim Pickens—asked me to work the barrel for him during the bull riding. Well, stupid old me! I told him yes, and now Maroncita's mad at me and will probably fire me after this three day rodeo is over. Turns out working the barrel is some dangerous. You gotta scrunch way down to keep the bull from reaching in with his long horns; and when the bull hits the barrel, one cowboy told me, it can pop the teeth right out of your head.*

Today, I met King Richards' daughter, Pam. He didn't

60

introduce us, of course; Maroncita did. Pam's not stuck up at all, but seems to think I'm cool. I didn't make a big play for her. You know me, Eddy. I gotta be careful not to break her heart. Ha! Ha!

The boy stopped along the racetrack to watch a bull-dogger make his run. It was Ruff Burleigh again. He spurred his horse out of the box behind the barrier, pounding his bay mare with a crop, hard on the tail of a horned steer, which leaped from a chute ahead of him. The steer was supposed to trigger a rubber barrier as he came out, but instead Burleigh's mare got a little eager and broke it with her chest, giving him a ten second penalty. On the off side of the steer, another cowboy galloped, hazing the steer into running straight.

Overtaking the steer, Ruff slid off his horse, gripping the steer by the horns, then sliding his right hand forward to get an arm lock on the beast's head. Braking the steer to a stop with his boot heels, the stout cowboy twisted him down with all four legs out straight, held him for the flagman's flag, then turned him loose.

"Four seconds flat," the announcer said, "but the judges have added on a ten second penalty, folks, for breaking the barrier. A tough break for the former All-Around Champion."

Angry with himself, Ruff picked up his crop, caught his mare and mounted, hitting her hard with the bat as he headed back across the arena and out behind the chutes.

The next bulldogger had better luck, dropping his steer in three point two seconds, the fastest time yet. The crowd came to its feet in applause.

Over beside the chutes, Lee could see Slim Pickens rolling

61

a stout red barrel along the ground. He stood it upright along the fence, then moved back to the chutes to help Jimmy Richards fill the chute with bulls for the bull riding.

He wished Maroncita would hurry. Only four more doggers on deck, and then she would be on. To pass the time he checked and rechecked her circingles and ran his fingers comblike through the mares' manes, straightening every hair. The last bulldogger was making his run when she came down out of the stands, where she had apparently been visiting some fans.

He had set up the jump all alone, and now she found fault with his work, went over and moved the heavy unit herself, two feet up the track and six inches to the left. He glanced over toward the chutes. The bulls were standing placidly in their stalls, and Slim had disappeared. The unknown bothered him; he wished the afternoon were over.

He helped Maroncita up on her horses. Standing on them tandem, one foot on a pad on the back of each horse, she circled them and headed down the track at a walk, then made her first jump, without fire, to get them used to the hurdle. As she circled and went back up the track for another jump, she nodded to Lee, giving him his cue. He drenched the asbestos cloth on the crossbar with white gasoline from a jug, then set it afire, stepping aside just as Maroncita turned her horses and came thundering down the track. Up in the stands someone screamed as the horses soared over the flames and went galloping on unscathed.

Quickly, as the fire burned itself out, Lee moved in and took down the hurdle; then, as Maroncita made her bows in front of the grandstand, he took her horses and hurried them back to her van.

He was off to report for duty at the chutes, when Slim

intercepted him. "Hey, Lee!" he said. "C'mere quick. I gotta do a job on that mug of yores." He led Lee to his trailer, where he painted the boy's face and loaned him a pair of baggy overalls and a wig made from the head of a mop. "Yew do a good job in that barrel," Slim said, "an' next time we may just come up with a better outfit."

Once they were in the arena, Slim rolled the red barrel out some forty feet from the chutes.

"Git down in there, Lee, an' try it fer size."

Lee swung his long legs over the sides. The bottom was nearly as open as the top. There were two cable handholds bound with electrician's tape along the sides, and wide shoulder straps so he could extend his legs through the bottom and walk, wearing the barrel like a suit of armor.

The youth hunkered down, taking hold of the grips.

"Further," Slim advised. "And git yore knees up to cradle yore chin. Thet's some better. Practice a few times so yew can drop in just one jump ahead of the bull."

He patted Lee on the back. "Thanks, an' good luck. Remember, whatever yew do, when thet ole bull is knockin' at yore door, fer heaven's sake don't stick yore head up to see who it is!"

The announcer called down to Slim. "Who's your partner this time, Slim?"

Slim looked up at Mel Lambert and grinned. "This here's a brand new one, Mel. Are yew ready fer this? Lee Oliver Rawls. Heck, Mel, thet's too much of a mouthful. Jes' call 'im Lee Overalls!"

Lee bridled a little, then grinned. They hadn't called him that name since he'd learned how to fight dirty in the fifth grade. But it was a stage name, just the way Slim Pickens was. And the further he could get from his real name, the safer he felt. *Maybe* he thought, *maybe it's all part of my fresh start.*

He sat on the rim of the barrel and waited. Nonchalantly, he looked along the fences and above the chute, hoping that Maroncita would appear among the contestants to watch him perform. He saw Jimmy's sister, Pam, sitting up above the chutes talking to the announcer, but she didn't seem to recognise him in his clown gear. Just beyond the fence, sitting on the hood of a tan pickup truck, was a handful of kids, sucking on bottles of cream soda. The caps were still on the bottles and he grinned, remembering one of the few bright spots in his childhood, when his mom had bought him a soda and made a tiny hole in the cap with a finishing nail to make the treat last all day.

A little girl in the bunch noticed him smiling and waved at him shyly. Lee grinned and waved back, deciding to put on a special act just for them. Standing up on the rim of the barrel, he held his nose as though the barrel were full of water and jumped in. Then he stuck one arm up over the rim and waved for help, as though he were drowning. When he peered up over the rim, the children were all giggling and feeling special.

Sometime I'm going to have kids like that, Lee thought to himself. *And that's how I'm going to make my kids feel. Special.*

There wasn't much more time to think. The first bull rider settled down on his ox. Slim came out wearing a matador's costume. He waved to the crowd as Mel Lambert stuck on a record, playing a short burst of frenzied, stirring bullfight music. Slim's features seemed to dissolve in a big, comic, toothy grin, then suddenly he was all business, sniffing hard to clear his nasal passages, looking to see what bull was next, and planning just how to handle him once he came out of the chute on the peck. There were few rodeo bulls in the West Slim didn't know by heart. He stood, cape ready, just a few feet from the barrel. It was his job to keep the cowboy from being gored or trampled, and he took the responsibility seriously.

The bull came bellowing out of the chute, whirling in a circle and kicking high, slinging his head. On the second jump, the rider went off over the bull's hips, and Slim moved in with his cape, sucking the bull away from the prostrate rider. He kept the cape between the bull's line of vision and his own body, so that the bull hit the cloth with his horns and missed the body of the clown. Just beyond the barrel, the bull swung around and took a stand.

"Git down, Lee!" Slim commanded. He tipped the barrel on its side and rolled it toward the bull. Lee clung to the handles as he listened for clues in the laughter of the crowd. Slim stood the barrel back on its end and tipped the open end of the barrel toward the bull as though to let him know someone was hiding inside. Lee looked out to see the face of the bull, shaking with anger, just inches away.

"Hang on, Lee!" Slim shouted. "Here he comes!"

The bull hit the barrel with explosive force. It seemed to Lee that the barrel was heading up into orbit, destined never to come down. But then it fell, and as it came down, the bull caught it on his horns and lofted it away again, catching it as it hit the earth and rolling it along the ground. Lee felt dizzy and sick to his stomach. But he had a quiet sort of faith that Slim wouldn't let the bull hurt him.

Slim stood the barrel upright, and Lee peered out over the rim, took off his hat, and sailed it at the bull. It caught the animal between the eyes, and the brahma charged at Slim's cape, hitting the barrel behind it with a sickening thump. When Lee peered out again, he heard the crowd applauding, and the bull was already halfway down the arena, trotting toward the catch pens.

"Yore doin' fine," Slim said. "Now put yore shoulders in the harness, let yore legs down and walk the barrel back into position fer the next bull."

"Well," Mel Lambert said. "That's Slim Pickens and his helper, Lee Overalls, folks. How do you like them so far?"

Lee felt the applause to his toes. Even better was the collective look of adulation on the kids on the hood of the pickup. They were his first fans, and he guessed that they would go home telling their parents about Lee Overalls.

By the time his old friend, Number Twelve, came out, Lee felt rashly confident. Maroncita and Pam were sitting visiting together in the announcer's stand, and Slim had even given him a friendly pat on the back with half the world watching. When Number Twelve came out bucking hard, Lee was standing just behind Slim, a dozen feet from his barrel, intending to lead the bull his way and dive into the barrel in the nick of time.

First jump out of the chute, the massive bull sent his rider sailing and whirled like a passing freight train through Slim's cape. The force of the blow jerked the clown into the bull's shoulder, and he slipped and went down. For one split second the boy froze in his tracks. The bull glanced at Lee then, as the crowd screamed, turned back toward his quarry on the ground. Suddenly Lee forgot his own fear; Slim was down and needed help. He could be seconds away from death. Lee leaped forward, slapped the startled bull across the nose, and drew his charge.

Number Twelve boiled up off Slim, caught Lee a punishing blow with one splintered horn, sending the boy reeling backwards, then followed through.

He hit me, Lee thought. *He hit me, and I didn't die!* He was suddenly calm, calculating. He danced backwards out of the bull's range. The horns missed him by centimeters, but they missed him. He knew he couldn't outrun the bull in a foot race, but if he took advantage of the bull's speed, he was sure he could out-maneuver him.

The bull hit him another sharp, glancing blow, but he straight-armed himself away, eluded the full thrust of the horns, and danced back past the bull's shoulders, towing the bull in a circle as he had seen Slim do. Out of the corner of his eye he could see the clown, on his feet now, limping but not hurt.

"Hyaah, bull!" Slim called, and the bull stopped in his tracks, looking first at the boy, then at the bullfighter advancing with his cape. He shook his head, backed up a few steps, pawed a shower of dirt over his hump, then gave up and went trotting off.

"Thanks, pal!" Slim said, wiping the dirt from his face.

Lee wanted to look up at the announcer's stand to see how Maroncita had taken all this, but he kept his eyes on the next chute and the next bull.

Compared to Number Twelve, the next ox was plumb gentle. He had petted this bull a number of times in the pen behind the chutes, scratched his long, drooping ears, and even picked him a whole armload of dandelion greens. The bull was his friend, and his dignity was important. So when the animal came flying his way, he made the bull look good, letting him chase and almost catch him as he scrambled in mock terror for the barrel. He vaulted in and vanished, as though scared out of his wits.

When he managed to peek up at the announcer's stand, Pam Richards and Mel Lambert were sitting there alone. Maroncita had vanished.

chapter twelve

❖

 owards midsummer, the pace seemed even more hectic as one rodeo seemed to butt up hard on the heels of another, with barely enough time in between for travel. Maroncita explained to Lee that since there were only so many good contestants available for any particular date, and only so much good bucking stock, rodeo committees did their best to select dates that didn't conflict with other major rodeos. But even so there were too many midsummer rodeos, and they would have to spend many a sleepless night on the road.

In the space of a few weeks, they worked sixteen rodeos. Fatigue showed in both their faces as they were caught up in the routine. One arena seemed the same as another. It was set up the van, care for the stock, set up props, help Maroncita perform, then off again for the next town. Just as life began to be monotonous, however, an event occurred that he would remember as long as he lived.

The old green Chevy truck didn't look like much when it drove up to the gate on the track and honked. The right window was half broken out and patched with cardboard; there were gravel splays on the windshield; on the driver's side, the door was stained with snoose juice spread into strangely artistic configurations by the slip stream. The running boards were caked with red and brown gumbo, while bleached tumbleweeds dragged from the front bumper. The honeycomb radiator was an entomologist's dream, an unmethodical collection of bumblebees, grasshoppers, dragonflies, darning needles, bee flies, moths, and butterflies, baked to permanence like flowers in the enamel of a dinner plate.

The driver was an old rancher, hair yellow-gray, peering out through stern, steel-rimmed spectacles from under a sweat-ringed gray flannel hat. In the back of the truck, precariously balanced, matching swaying rhythms with the rickety racks, was one lone black draft horse, with what looked like magpie nests of dead sagebrush and juniper in his mane and tail.

"Where's Mister Richards?" the old man shouted above the din of the engine as Lee opened the gate.

Lee jerked his thumb toward the corrals, where King and his satellites were wrapping burlap strips around the horns of some roping steers. Lee followed the slow progress of the truck on foot, curious about the big horse.

King Richards saw the truck coming and hastened to meet it.

"Mister Richards," the old man said, turning off the ignition. The engine refused to die, popping and sputtering as

70

the heat made a mirage above the hood, and the whole wreck took on a sideways shimmy instead of a forward one. A bang from the rusted-through muffler put the old relic out of its misery, leaving everyone standing in a pool of startled silence.

The tall man acknowledged his identity and came closer.

"Name's Bart Shelley," the man said. "Got half a good young work team here; t'other half got shot by jacklighters. Have a hunch he might just make a bucking horse." There was a twinkle in the old man's eye that intimated he knew more about the horse's ability than he let on. "You want me to unload him?"

"Bart! Bart!" King smiled. "Yuh old scoundrel. Yuh think I don't know this old black horse?" He stepped back for a good look. "Why that's Blackhawk, Bart. Fifteen years ago every rodeo contractor in the country was tryin' tuh buy this hoss, and yuh wouldn't sell. Tuh my mind he was as great as Five Minutes Till Midnight. Once in a while you'd run him in some little Indian rodeo, but then we'd start pesterin' yuh fer him all over again and yuh'd open the gate to the corral and two minutes later he'd just be a memory. I can tell yuh now, I hankered fer thet hoss more than I ever hankered fer eny woman."

"He ain't never been hurt, King. Give him a try. Let some of yore good boys on him an' I guarantee he'll buck 'em down."

"I don't want tuh buy him," King said. "Ef yuh sold thet hoss, Bart, yuh'd be dead before the' ink was dry on the contract."

"You don't understand, King. There was just three things in my life meant somethin'. My wife, Effie, my ranch, and Blackhawk. Five years ago, Effie took sick from the cancers,

71

an' she took a long an' painful time a-dyin'. Sometimes I don't know why the Lord does things thet way. The ranch went to pay the bills, but she made me promise never to sell Blackhawk as long as she lived. Well, I got to now, King. I'll sell the old hoss to you fer jus' what it takes to give Effie a decent burial. OK?"

"I'm not about to buy thet ol' hoss from yuh, Bart. Yuh go give yore wife the good and decent funeral she deserves, and then yuh hev them people send the bill tuh King Richards.

"An we'll give old Blackhawk a try, because he was a great hoss and deserves the reputation in history yuh never let 'im have. I'll hev tuh see 'im buck once tuh make sure he's still spry enough to do the job. And when yuh get yore business taken care of, Bart, I want yuh tuh come back here an' take care of yore old hoss, hear?"

King Richards looked over at Lee. "What about it, kid. Feel like tryin' one today?"

Lee nodded, feeling somehow that it was simply a case of destiny, all the players having been brought here at this appointed time.

The old man started the truck engine to galloping again, then rammed the old wreck into reverse, trying to sight the unloading chute in the wild vibrations of the mirror. As the man backed the truck toward the chute, Lee peered in through the slats. The horse's hooves were big and splintered, and feathers choked with cockleburs hung from his fetlocks. His eyes were big and black, his brow prominent, the nose Roman, his look untamed by age. As the truck bumped finally against the chute, his snort of alarm was like the backfire of a diesel engine.

The old man didn't go up in the truck with him; instead he hobbled up to the side of the rack, untied the rope from the

72

outside, and tossed it over the animal's neck, letting him go thumping down the chute by himself. Big as the animal was, he came out like a cat out of a box trap, working nervously up and down the corral fence, testing the planks with his chest.

Jimmy opened a gate and let him into the chutes, then went to the van and came back with the saddle Lee had used before. A handful of cowboys, though tired from the day's activities, came out of their trailers to watch the action.

Lee was relieved to see Slim among them. The clown squinted at the new horse, reading his history. "Collar marks on 'im," Slim mused, "but his roach job's growed out a long time ago. Look in his eye, he's an old runaway. Wish I had a dollar fer every wagon he tore up when he was young. Spent more time out on the range than he ever spent in a corral. An' the inside of a barn would plumb frighten 'im to death." He turned to the old man. "Right, Mister?"

The old man spat a lip of grasshopper juice into the dust, then smiled. "Jest about," he said.

Slim looked at Lee. "Goin' tew try 'im?"

The boy nodded.

"Well, yore a glutton fer punishment. Let me tell yew somethin'; I'd charge thet King Richards a fifty tew try this one."

The clown picked up Lee's saddle and carried it into the arena.

"Sure yew want 'im, Lee? Better let me take a settin' on 'im. I owe yew one."

The boy shook his head. There was something about the animal that had gripped him ever since he had first seen him in the truck.

Friend Eddy, he said to himself. *I suppose I don't have*

*brain one getting on this big lunker, but I gotta try, Eddy.
I just gotta try.*

"Lee," Slim said as they saddled the big black. "Yew never asked fer my advice, but I'm goin' tew give it anyway. This hoss has been around awhile, but my guess is he's a keg a black powder. He's big and strong, with one of the longest barrels on 'im I've seen on a bronc. Try to tight leg 'im an' he'll fair ta bust yew loose from yer skin fer shore. Just kick yerself loose an' try to balance 'im, lettin' 'im tow yew along by the rein. If yew ask me, it's yer best chance of makin' a ride."

The big cowboy slid the saddle ahead. "We'll set the saddle up high on the withers tew take some of the snap out of his back. I'll take care of the flank strap myself, snug but not too tight. Yew got thet, Lee?"

He nodded, measured off his rein, and marked it with a wisp of mane hair stuck into the weave.

"He's been in the chute before, I reckon," Slim said. "Look at his eye. Not a bit of fear!"

Lee looked at him and smiled. For once he knew more about an animal than Slim.

Standing on the chute gate, his feet ached, and his knees began to jump with nervous tension. Taking his rein, he looked out for a moment into the arena, making sure King Richards was ready. Old Bart Shelley stood on the ground, well up the chutes, his eyes twinkling in anticipation.

"Ready?" Jimmy Richards asked, and Lee nodded his head.

The big black came out fast and had already bucked two big jumps when he gained the arena. With a squeal of rage, he chased a cowboy along the chutes, then powered upward and kicked, showering dirt over the spectators, hit the ground

74

with a jolt, then slanted away to the right, almost knocking old Bart down. Standing on his hind legs, the horse seemed to be coming over backwards, but instead he soared into another dive, now standing with his head between his front legs, hind feet kicking high, the cantle scraping hide from Lee's back, now rearing on his hind legs and once more leaping heaven bound.

Lee kicked himself loose, letting the swells of the saddle jerk between his knees, spurring to keep his balance, letting the rein tow him through the air. His jaw clamped hard in his determination to ride. He saw the horse's feet move out and plant themselves to the left, and braced himself for a spin to the right. There was no fancy contesting involved. All he had to do was show King that the animal could still buck.

The horse kicked at the moon, jerked his head hard, then slung it back, throwing slack into the rein as he tried to bite Lee's leg. No wild, freak jumps here, just hard, honest, jolting leaps, no two the same, each getting more difficult than the one before. Lee kept his feet forward, taking as much of the jolt with the stirrups as he could.

As though afraid now that Lee might finish his ride, King moved in swiftly, galloping up alongside the bronc, grabbing Lee around the shoulders, pulling him out of the saddle. Lee kept spurring in the air, not realizing that the ride was over. When Blackhawk reached the end of the arena, he was still popping the stirrups over his back.

Slim was out there when the man lowered the boy to the ground.

"Yew moved in mighty fast, King." Slim grinned. "Like maybe yew wanted tew make sure the boy didn't get him rode."

King didn't answer. Another time he might have bridled a

little at the remark. Now he had other things on his mind. The great horse Blackhawk, at long last, was about to begin his professional career. He was already twenty-four years old, an age when most other saddle broncs had long since retired.

That night, Lee was so weary he scarcely touched the food Maroncita set before him. She sat at a small table just off the kitchen area, mending a tear in one of her costumes. He wanted to tell her how he'd ridden the big black, to tell her about the old man and his love for his horse, his wife, and the ranch he was losing to the bank. He opened his mouth, determined to make some words come, but nothing happened. He rose from the table, went outdoors, and stood in the darkness. Gingerly, he touched his throat. He could feel nothing wrong. Whatever swelling had been there from the blow of the bull's horn had long been gone. The sounds just wouldn't come.

Down by the chutes, the lights were still on, and King and the old man were still down there visiting, fussing over that black horse.

He turned away and found his bedroll in the dark. During the night, he heard the sound of the old truck backfiring as it started up and watched as the headlights jerked along the dusty road and pooled in a chalk bank as the truck gained the main highway. For a long time the transmission ground along in low, then second, then third, and finally the sound faded out forever as the old Chevy crossed into another valley and was gone.

chapter
thirteen

t seemed to Lee that he had never seen more beautiful
country. He sat up front in the van as Maroncita drove
on and on, matching his silence with her own. They left the
great rolling eastern plains—the soft strips of green alter-
nating with the brown of summer fallow ground, the pastel
pinks of distant plateaus, the shimmering hazes of summer
heat—and moved up into the Rockies, where patches of dark
forest under brilliant skies fought for toeholds on magnificent but tortured escarpments of rock.

They were headed for yet another King Richards rodeo
in the northern part of the state.

Before they left the last place, Lee had been a little hurt
to come back from helping Maroncita with her stock, to find
that Slim Pickens had already loaded his horse, mule, wife,
and child and pulled out, and there wasn't so much as a
whisper of hay where his trailer had stood. Then on the way

back to Maroncita's van, he had happened to overhear a conversation between two other cowboys that indicated that Slim and his retinue had headed south into Wyoming for a week of fishing before his next rodeo and wouldn't be back making one of King's shows for a month. Lee wondered if Slim's former barrel man would catch up with him and go back to working the barrel.

Some experience was better than no experience, and Lee hoped that somewhere up the line another clown would give him another chance. And besides the experience, Lee had accumulated some savings, the first in his lifetime, carefully pinned in a hidden pocket in his shirt.

As he sat enjoying the scenery, he rubbed his throat, wishing that his voice would come back. He would have enjoyed talking to Maroncita. There were all sorts of questions about rodeo he wanted to ask.

Friend Eddy, he mused, thirsting for a conversation, *I guess you'd be surprised that noisy old me can't talk any more. I open my mouth, Eddy, but nothing comes. There are times when it's kind of nice to be silent, times when I'm sure Maroncita gives me credit for more sense than I've got, but there are times like right now, when I've got her all to myself, when I'd like to do more than just sit here like a lump.*

I sure do like this life, Eddy. It is a fresh start. At a couple of rodeos I did some clowning and barrel work with Slim Pickens, the famous clown. I even managed to pull a bull off him that was working him over something awful. Two or three of these people seem to have a grudge against me, but the rest are starting to be friendly. Slim went out of his way to teach me things, and Maroncita—well, she's something special.

Lee's thoughts were interrupted by a small flock of snow-white mountain goats, browsing far up the side of a rocky cliff. He touched Maroncita's arm and pointed.

"Hey!" she said. "Look at those. Let me pull over and stop. I've never seen a mountain goat before, though I've made this drive a jillon times."

She parked off the shoulder of the road, disappeared back into the van, and brought out a pair of field glasses. Leaning back against the vehicle to steady herself, she watched them intently; at the same time, Lee found he could study her unobserved. The warm summer wind flowing through the canyon fluttered the soft hair along her temples like yellow butterflies trying to get out.

"Look!" she cried. "They've got babies with them. Oh, Lee! Look!" She handed him the glasses.

He took the binoculars from her, feeling traces of her warmth in the steel. They were the first he had ever used, and he had no idea how to focus them. The goats were white blurs in the distance, but he wasn't about to fumble with the knobs and show her how inexperienced he was. He handed them back just as the goats moved past a rocky cornice and were gone.

As they drove further back into the mountains, they descended a long ridge into a narrow river valley, whose green meadows were covered with wildflowers. There were so many, Lee wondered who had planted them there, then flushed, realizing that they were wild. Further up the valley, a mountain stream coursed down out of a pine forest in a series of waterfalls and passed under the highway. Maroncita parked the van in a meadow, and together they unloaded the horses to rest and water them. After a steady diet of dry hay, the mares went crazy for the lush, green forage.

"It's so beautiful, Lee," Maroncita said. "If you'd like to

79

go with me, we could go for a ride up through the woods to the top of that ridge. Each of us could ride one horse and lead another; that way they would all get some exercise."

He gave her a pleased smile. They saddled up, Maroncita riding Jezebel and leading Blondie, Lee riding Tune, leading Breeze. Together they rode up through alpine forests, now and then letting their horses catch their wind and graze on the rich mountain grasses.

Two hours later, they came to the broad summit of the ridge and looked back down from their vantage point; the van looked like a tiny brown toy, and the highway like a piece of some little girl's hair ribbon lost in the grass. To Lee it seemed, suddenly, as if his past was far away. The nightmares of living in tenements, forced by his stepfather, Slick, to steal. The hunger gnawing at his stomach. The fear of being caught by the police with stolen property and sent to reform school. Fear of walking alone without his gang to protect him. Fear of dying a violent death. Now he sat on a beautiful mare, beside a beautiful woman, in a beautiful land. A full belly, money in his pocket that he'd earned by his own hand, and nothing to be afraid of. He felt like an eagle, soaring over a broad wild kingdom, piercing eyes taking it all in to the smallest detail, owning all of it, yet owning none of it.

You'd never believe this country, Eddy, he mused. *A city like San Francisco could fit in its back pocket. I never realized that this land existed; sure, I saw pictures of it now and then in books or store windows, but they never expressed how BIG things are.*

I don't even feel like the same person I was. Once you told me, Eddy, that you hated stealing. I didn't understand then what you meant, I never knew much else. Well, I've learned some things, Eddy, and the only way Slick could take me back is—well—dead.

A pale orange hawk went rocketing below them on pointed wings. He had seen hawks from below before, but never from above. It made him dizzy to watch, and he turned away.

It was late afternoon before they managed to work their tired horses down the ridges to the van.

"We're late," Maroncita said, "but it's worth it. Two hundred and eighty more miles to go, and a performance tomorrow afternoon, but what an experience!" Her face glowed with pleasure.

Lee dozed off in the front seat of the van. Hours later he awoke to find her still behind the wheel, driving steadily north. Now and then lights from an oncoming vehicle would catch her face, and her dangling earrings would twinkle like tiny stars. She was so beautiful that he lay there pretending sleep, hoping for another set of car lights to stab the darkness.

It was after midnight when they arrived at their destination. Drugged with sleep, Lee staggered out to help Maroncita take care of the horses. That night as he stretched out in his bedroll among the mares, he lay for a few moments looking up at the northern sky. It looked brighter maybe, and a bit closer than at the last town, but it was the one constant left in his life.

Not far away, he could see a pen full of rodeo broncs, among them some old friends, Yellow Fever and beside him the newest horse, Blackhawk. The yellow horse dropped his head to feed in a manger, but Blackhawk stood with head high, nostrils flared, looking south as though dreaming of some far-off rimrock range on which he had been born.

81

Somewhere in the darkness beyond the pale of yellow lights, a lovesick mare nickered and was answered by a stallion; a cow bawled softly to her calf. Lee laid his head down upon his pillow and slept.

The early morning air in the Montana mountains was pure and sweet, but chill. Lee pulled the blankets of the bedroll close about his bare shoulders and lay there, luxuriating in warmth and the smell of pines, happy to be alive. Jezebel, the mean mare, seemed to sense that he was awake and nickered to him for attention; and the other animals, taking a cue from her, looked over at him expectantly, pawing the ground, impatient to be fed.

Okay, you gals, he thought. *So you won't let a guy sleep in. You want your breakfast, do you?* He struggled from his bedroll, put on his Levi's, did a series of strenuous muscle-building exercises, then finished dressing and gave each of them a nosebag of grain.

It was still early when he finished his chores, so he strolled across to the corrals where the bucking horses were kept and climbed in with them. He held out his hand to Blackhawk.

The big horse snorted, but calmed down quickly, then came a couple of steps forward, holding out his nose to sniff at him. Lee cupped his hand first over one eye then the other, scratching the horse's lids. Blackhawk snuffled in contentment, wrinkled his nose, yawned, baring his yellow teeth, ground up one last remnant of hay between his molars, tossed his nose as though to dislodge a fly, then lowered his head to be scratched.

"Gee, you're awfully brave to be doing that, or else you're a darn fool." Pam Richards's voice came from directly behind him. He glanced over his shoulder to see her sitting on her barrel racing mare.

"My brother Jimmy's scared to death of that horse," she went on. "Said Blackhawk bared his teeth at him the other day, laid back his ears, and ran him clear up over the corral fence."

Lee swelled up a little and draped one arm over the big horse's neck, leaning against his heavy shoulder. The big, long-bodied horse yawned, as though bored.

"Cita says you've got a way with horses; says you're a natural and do things right by instinct. And Slim, he says you've got a lot of guts, and what with a good sense of balance, you might be quite a bronc rider some day."

Lee flushed at the compliments, but busied himself straightening out a tangle in the black horse's mane.

"Daddy's going to put Blackhawk and Yellow Fever in the bronc riding today. You ought to sign up. You could ride either of them if you really tried. Slim said you had Blackhawk rode when my dad moved in and pulled you off his back. You could ride them, Lee, couldn't you?"

Lee glanced at the girl and shrugged. The gesture meant yes or maybe no, but mainly, of course. His hand pressed hard against his shirt pocket where he hid his money. Enough there for entrance fees. It was an idea at that. One trouble, though, was that he didn't have an association saddle.

She seemed to read his thoughts, carrying on the conversation just as though he'd answered her. "Dad keeps some extra saddles in the tack van for contestants," she said. "Please sign up! I watched you trying out saddle broncs and you have lots of style. I'd be so proud of you if you won!"

Lee was mulling it over in his mind when Jimmy Richards noticed that Pam was talking to him and came charging up ahorseback.

"You!" he snapped at Pam. "Better be more particular who yuh talk tuh, young miss. Get over to the trailer! Dad wants his breakfast right now!"

Pam's face turned scarlet and her mouth opened to retort, but she thought better of it and reined her mare away.

Jimmy looked hard at Lee, who stood beside Blackhawk, his arm still draped across the big outlaw's neck. "And you," he said. "Get away from those saddle broncs. Yuh got no business in there with 'em!"

If Lee had any doubts about what he was going to do, they faded there and then. "I'll show that guy," he thought. "I'll sign up for the saddle broncs because I've got a sneaking suspicion he's scared to. And the bull riding too, because he's not that good, and there's just the chance I could beat him at his own game!"

He let Blackhawk eat a little grain from his cupped hand, and the big horse nosed the pocket of his jacket for more.

"I said, 'Get away from those horses,'" Jimmy snapped, his face crimson with anger.

Lee sauntered over to the fence, laid a hand on the top rail, and vaulted over. He picked up a splinter in his hand doing it, but it was worth it. He'd been practicing on fences ever since Maroncita had showed him how to vault on a horse's back. He went back to the van, applied a Band-Aid to his wound, and finished his chores.

The rodeo secretary glanced at him curiously as he plunked two crisp fifty dollar bills down on the desk and pointed out the two events he wanted to enter. When his money had vanished into the cash box, and he was walking back to eat breakfast with Maroncita, he felt foolish. He had about as much chance of getting his entrance fees back in those riding events as sprouting wings and flying. What a way to throw his money away! Then he thought of Jimmy Richards, and his jaw set. Win or lose, he was going to try. He might be bucked off a few horses and bulls at first, but someday he was going to be a contender!

As he walked, he tried to remember everything Slim had taught him about setting his saddle, measuring off his rein, watching down the left shoulder for the horse's hooves or adjusting the flank.

"A good flanker," Slim had said, "could buck a man off or let him steal a ride."

Maroncita was cooking breakfast when he arrived. Through the open window of the van, he could hear bacon snapping and crackling in the frying pan. He sat down on a block of wood and leaned back against the van with the morning sun on his face and tried to imagine what it would be like to be married to her and not just her hired man.

When he sat down at the table, he longed to take a pencil and paper and tell her that he had decided to compete, and maybe even get rid of some of his fears by joking about them. But then he sensed that the news wasn't going to please her.

All morning he slaved, polishing her equipment to high luster, currying her mares until they glowed, not a hair out of place. He checked the latigos on her saddles and circingles, replacing those that were worn. Maroncita glanced at him curiously, but she didn't comment.

That afternoon, Lee watched Pam Richards make a nearly faultless run in the barrel racing, winning the day money and setting a time that was an arena record.

She walked her mare over to where he stood, her pretty face beaming with happiness. "Pretty good, huh?" She grinned at him. "This old mare was fair to flying out there today." She reined up beside him, reaching down to pat the animal's neck. "It's going to be a good day for us both. I can't wait to watch you ride." She leaned forward in her saddle and reached to straighten the black's foretop. "I see you drew Top Rail. He's that little roan horse, you know. Dad says he's a pretty fair draw. There's been some money won on him, and you can always count on him to put on a good show for the judges. He's put some pretty good cowboys on the ground, but you can ride him, Lee. I just know you can."

Top Rail! He'd watched the horse buck a number of times and thought maybe he knew his tricks. Fast and crooked, but he had a back kick that was as regular as clockwork. Not like Blackhawk, where every jump came from somewhere else, and if you tried to guess at the next jump you were wrong. If only he could pick up the rhythm with Top Rail and keep it up for ten seconds!

He wished he had been in the office when they drew his name out of the hat and had seen the look on that Jimmy Richards's face. The secretary had wanted him to sign his real name, but he didn't want to chance it being published in the local press along with the other contestants. It was too small a world. Someone who knew him in the old days might just happen to see it and mention it in a letter to Slick in prison. If Slick was out to get him, then even Montana wasn't too far for his murderous arm to reach.

And so he had signed his name as Lee Overalls. He found a program tacked to the chutes, ran his finger down the list, and there it was! "Lee Overalls on Top Rail." He traced his finger down the list of bull riders, and there it was again, opposite bull Number Twelve. Good! He'd drawn Number Twelve again! The bull was tough, but at least he was a known quantity. He was a lot stronger now than he had been when he arrived, and with Maroncita's good cooking, he'd filled out a little too. He shivered in his excitement. He was going to give it one whale of a try.

He helped Maroncita with her trick riding performance. The audience was a lot smaller than usual, but they weren't afraid to applaud. When she was done, he led her horses back to the van; then once the horses were cared for, he hurried over to the chutes, where Jimmy was just moving the saddle broncs up into the bucking chutes. Lee pitched in to help unbidden, slamming the cross gate on each horse as it moved up into the proper slot.

Once the horses were in, he handed Jimmy a note asking to borrow a bronc saddle. Jimmy didn't look pleased, but he jerked his thumb toward a pile of saddles lying by the end of the chutes.

"Take one of those," he said. "There are some bronc reins hanging on the fence. See that you put 'em back."

Top Rail turned his head as Lee approached and nickered to him. Only the other day he'd slipped the little roan an apple from his lunch, and the horse seemed to remember. He reached in and scratched the animal beneath the chin. "Maybe he'll take good care of me out there," he thought.

He picked out a saddle that looked familiar, adjusted the stirrups, then settled it carefully, well up on the horse's withers, fished a wisp of roan mane out from under the forks of the saddle, hooked the cinch ring, shoved the latigo through and tightened it up. He couldn't make himself watch as the first bronc rider came out on a big dapple gray and made it to the whistle.

"And now, out of Chute Number Two, a young cowboy named Lee Overalls, who drew that good little bucking horse from Oregon, Top Rail."

Lee took his rein and settled down on the roan, searching out the narrow stirrups with his toes. He nodded to Jimmy and the gate swung open. As the horse turned, he seemed to hear Slim's voice, "Yew c'n do it, kid! Git yore toes out, an' yore spurs in his neck to start 'im, then write yore name on the cantle." But then he seemed to hear Slim's good-natured aside to someone watching. "Yew know whut? I'll tell yew somethin'! Thet gol-dang Lee's got everythin' it takes tew ride thet horse—except the ability."

The little horse disappeared beneath the swells of the saddle; the cantle popped him hard on the seat, but he leaned back against it, jerking his spurs back in long, smooth strokes. Every time the horse's front feet hit the ground, Lee shoved his stirrups forward to take the jolt. He rode easily, using balance instead of strength, letting Top Rail tow him along with the rein. The horse was fast, high-bucking, and showy, but without the spine-jolting crashes of a Blackhawk.

Halfway across the arena, he hit the horse unevenly with his spurs and threw Top Rail into a spin. He kept trying to

89

spur, but the inside leg didn't seem to want to move. He'd taken his rein a little long, and with the spin, his rein hand was somewhere back of his ear, much higher in the air than felt comfortable.

Top Rail straightened out and bucked back toward the chutes, scattering cowboys along the fence. The bronc's hind feet kicked high, firing clods of dirt up into the announcer's stand. Suddenly, there was the whistle, the pickup men hammered in alongside, and a stout arm moved around his shoulders as a rider reined his horse to the left and swung him away from the plunging bronc.

The crowd applauded, not loudly, but politely. The judges conferred with each other, then made pencil tracks on their clipboards, scoring so much for the horse, so much for the rider. He walked slowly back to the chute, eyes focused intently on the ground as though looking for a wallet. Then there was Mel Lambert's voice. He was tied with the other rider for first place. He hoped that Maroncita was listening. How astonished she'd be!

Then he remembered she'd probably not associate the name Lee Overalls with her hired man.

In two wicked jumps, Blackhawk bucked off a good cowboy from Alberta, and Yellow Fever lost his rider just out of the chute.

Lee's hopes began to rise, but just then Ruff Burleigh came out of the chute, cigarette hanging, spurring like a madman, riding a big sorrel named Snake, who was definitely having a good day.

The judges liked Ruff's ride and might just as well have handed him a check for first place right then and there.

The next horse was a big, hairy brute named Mastadon,

who looked like a throwback to prehistory. Just before the whistle, he jettisoned his rider, hurling him against an arena gate, breaking the cowboy's leg. There was an air of subdued silence as an ambulance drove into the arena, and two attendants rolled the contestant onto a stretcher, loaded him, and drove him off to a hospital. Lee's hopes soared as the next two cowboys were bucked off, but then two rode well and scored higher than Lee. He ended up the day tied for fourth place, in the day money.

Still, he was pleased. When Maroncita came out to do her fire jump, he hoped she would congratulate him. Instead she ignored him, except to give him a few final instructions on where to place the hurdle.

Making her approach, she lost her concentration, slipped, and fought for balance as her mounts smacked shoulders, then lurched apart. She swayed, and for one agonizing moment, Lee thought she was going to fall between the galloping mares and be trampled, but a split second before they soared over the flaming jump, she got the rhythm, recovered, and landed smoothly, racing off with them down the track.

She thundered past him, angry with herself, letting her two horses run themselves out on the track, then took them through a gate beyond the grandstand area to her van. There was no time for Lee to help her since the bull riding was on.

Jimmy made a careful ride on a racehorse of a bull. He made it to the whistle, but was marked low. The next five riders all drew tough bulls and ended up in the dirt. That left Lee in the position of spoiler.

As he mounted the chutes, he wished Slim were out there with his cape to take care of him. The two clowns who had contracted this show were good, but not in Slim's class. Lee

91

climbed over the top plank, leaned to take his loose-rope, settled down on the big, black brahma, took his wraps, and signaled the gate man to open up and let him meet his destiny.

He was braver now than he was when he first tried Number Twelve. He rode out the first part of the storm easily, leaning way back from the arc of those wildly swinging horns. On the fourth jump, the clanging bell under the bull seemed to change pitch as the bull went into a spin. The bull threw some wild, dirty, head-clinging leaps, but still Lee managed to hang on. Just as the whistle blew, however, his strength seemed to evaporate, and his mucles turned to milk. His hand lost its grip on the bull rope, and the bull rushed on without him.

It was close. The judges held a conference as to whether or not the boy had made it to the whistle. Beside himself with tension, Jimmy paced the chutes, trying to anticipate the decision by watching the faces of the judges. Lee himself didn't know. He thought that maybe he'd qualified, but he wasn't going to argue one way or another. He turned his back on the judges and walked toward the chutes.

When he glanced up at the announcer's stand, he saw Pam beating her hands in applause, her face radiant with excitement. He assumed that she was clapping for her brother Jimmy, then suddenly Mel Lambert's voice sunk in. He had scored eight points higher than Jimmy Richards.

But there were two more bull riders to go. He kept himself busy along the chutes, helping with the bull ropes and the flanks. One of the riders was disqualified for touching his bull with his free hand; the other twisted his ankle in the chutes, and the bull came out without him.

When Mel Lamber announced the result of the day's bull riding, Lee Overalls was in first place, Jimmy Richards was in second, with the balance of the bull riding purse split on the ground among the remaining entrants.

chapter fifteen

That night Lee slept badly. The pressures of being first in the bull riding gnawed at him. If he had been more confident of his ability, perhaps he could have relaxed. As he lay in his bedroll, he wondered what ox he would draw and pictured himself flying off any number of bulls. Then he began to worry about saddle broncs. He was tied for fourth place. If he managed to draw either Blackhawk or Yellow Fever, and Ruff Burleigh got bucked off, as he sometimes did—

He finally conquered the rodeo worries only to be upset by night noises. The rustling of Maroncita's horses as they nosed their hay, snuffling contentedly, then chewing endlessly, molar grinding on molar. Someone's stallion pawing the floorboards of a horse van, nickering a love song to every mare on the place. Trucks on the nearby highway, shifting downward for a stoplight, then up again through a wide range of gears. A cowboy snoring from his bedroll a hundred feet away. And the moon playing at being a cold, heatless sort of sun, bathing the rodeo grounds with ghostly light.

He was glad when morning came. He raised up on an elbow, squinting at his watch, then heard someone clear his throat behind him and turned his head to see Jimmy Richards standing there.

"We've got some more broncs to try out," Jimmy said. "That is, if yuh ain't too big fer yore britches now. The old man wants tuh git at 'em early, afore things git busy with the rodeo. Yuh want in?"

Lee nodded. Maybe they planned to wear him down, or get him hurt, to give Jimmy more of a chance. But he knew he needed the practice. Every horse he came out on increased his confidence, and if the bronc happened to be good enough to make the Richards's sting, he already had one jump on the other cowboys because he'd already taken a setting on the animal.

He got up, washed his face in an enameled basin of icy water, and poured it out over the dust. He shivered as he put on his shirt, though it may have been as much from excitement as from the cool mountain air. Maroncita's mares nickered to him. *You girls don't want my company*, he thought, *just some food*. He ambled over to them, slapping them affectionately on their broad, silk-smooth rumps, careful to give each animal the same amount of attention. The mean mare, Jezebel, cocked a foot at him out of habit, but he grinned at her, crowded close to her legs, and slapped her anyway.

Slim had taught him that. "Crowd close, then if they kick yew, they can't get in much of a swing."

Now and then the mare tried to bluff him out, popping that foot his way just to keep him honest. Sometimes, however, when he sat on a bale of hay reading *Hoofs and Horns*, a rodeo magazine, she'd work at her knots until she got them untied, then leave the other horses to come over and stand near him, half asleep, one hind leg cocked out of habit against enemies, lower lip drooping, eyes half closed, as though pretending not to look at him. Now that was love!

Friend Eddy, he thought. *Why don't you show up here? You ought to see the way your old buddy is riding saddle broncs and bulls. I'm not very excited about becoming a bull rider. I'd like always to be able to eat corn on the cob. I just signed up for the bull riding to get Jimmy's goat.*

You might not even recognise me. I musta shot up a coupla inches since I came here, what with lots of good food, plenty of sleep, and exercise. And I'm getting muscles like a black-smith. I carry a rubber ball around with me and squeeze it every chance I get. Then too, 'bout every one of these rodeo arenas has a racetrack, so I get in lots of jogging. I'm getting too tall to be a good bull rider. But lots of saddle bronc riders are tall and slender.

Boy, would you ever be surprised, Eddy, if I got to be Saddle Bronc Riding Champion of the World. You might be way down there in Mexico and see my name and picture in the paper and say "Hey, that guy looks familiar. Saints be preserved! That's got to be my old buddy, Lee. Lee Over-alls?" Ha, Ha, Eddy. That's just a nickname they gave me around the rodeos.

I just got to thinking, Eddy. I don't want to get famous.

96

What if Slick got out of the pen and was lying in a motel somewhere and saw my picture on the Late Show, or in a newspaper, and got an idea where to find me? Maybe once you and I, Eddy, we were just meal tickets to Slick. But we know enough about him to hang him. He'd kill us both if he had the chance.

I hate not being able to talk, Eddy. It's real lonesome. First money I put together riding rough stock, I'm going to head for the office of a good doctor and get my throat checked out. It's tough to visit with these guys around here when you got to write everything down. Looking at the bright side, Slim says, "if a feller can talk, he don't need to know how to spell." Well, I gotta go now, Eddy. I can hear the boss lady up and around in her van. Wish you could see her; she's sure beautiful!

After breakfast, Lee went over to the corrals, where a stock truck was unloading horses. There were fifteen broncs to try out, and he hoped he wouldn't have to come out of the chute on all of them.

Jimmy looked sullen, and his father seemed to be in a real storm. He figured they must be having a quarrel. He wondered what it would be like to have a fight with your real dad. His own father had died when he was about three; after that had come a succession of guys, none of whom had stuck around long in his life. And then came Slick. He'd been bad news right from the start.

Lee had ridden four of the horses out of the chutes, none of them keepers, when King Richards rode up on his horse.

"Jimmy," he snapped. "I tole yuh! Yore goin' tuh ride saddle broncs or leave home! Now git wunna them saddles on a green bronc an' git yoreself sum practice!"

"Like hell I will!" Jimmy shot back.

"This here's yore last chance, boy!" King growled.

Lee turned his back on the argument and busied himself saddling his next horse, a big bay. When he looked up from setting his flank strap, Jimmy had taken a saddle and was setting it down on a horse in the next chute.

Lee made his ride. The horse felt good beneath him; he got the rhythm and practiced spurring, raking him high behind. The horse bucked harder and harder, gaining confidence, and Lee had a feeling King might keep him for his string.

When he got back to the chutes, Jimmy was having trouble with his horse. The animal kept fighting the chute, snorting in fear. Lee glanced at Jimmy and couldn't believe his eyes. Jimmy was plumb scared, and probably the horse could smell it.

Lee climbed the chute and laid one hand on the animal's neck, stroking him, and the animal quieted some. Then he crossed over to the catwalk behind the chute to take hold of Jimmy's belt in case the horse reared and came over backwards in the chute.

"Git yore hands offa me!" Jimmy shouted. He took his rein and lowered himself slowly, reluctantly, feet jumping with tension as he searched for the stirrups with the toes of his boots. His face was green with fear, and sweat made a dark stain down the back of his blue shirt.

The horse tensed under the weight and kicked backwards with both hind feet, rattling the gate.

That poor horse is as scared as he is! Lee thought. *He'd better get out on him fast.*

Jimmy never had a chance. Suddenly the horse exploded in the chute and came over backwards. The boy didn't try to save himself, just submitted to Fate, like someone with a death wish, as the horse carried him over backwards. Too late, Lee grabbed for his belt but missed. The gate man opened the gate, and the horse rolled over, got to his feet, and went off bucking across the arena, empty stirrups popping above the saddle.

"Yuh do thet a-purpose, boy?" King Richards shouted, his face livid with anger. He didn't even bother to get off his horse. Jimmy lay a crumpled heap in the chute. But he was conscious. His look never left his father, as though the whole thing had been King's fault.

"Yuh let 'im do it to yuh!" King raged. "Better git up offen the ground an' walk, yuh hear? An' yuh keep walkin'. I don't want no yella-livered coward 'roun here!"

Jimmy closed his eyes in pain, and a tear squeezed from his lids to course down over one dusty cheek, mingling with blood where the rough planks had scraped off hide. Lee knew the boy wasn't faking. He was hurt bad. Covering Jimmy with his jacket to keep him warm against shock, he ran to get Maroncita.

When she came to the door of her van, she had only to glance at Lee's face to know there had been an accident. She grabbed some blankets and ran with him to the chute. When they got there, Pam was helping a couple of cowboys with a stretcher put her brother into a station wagon. Maroncita uttered a little cry, but she steeled herself and took over.

"You!" she said to one of the cowboys. "Jump in and get these blankets over him. Pam and I will ride with him. And you!" she said to the other. "Turn the heater up high and drive like hell for that hospital!"

Lee helped Pam into the wagon and turned to take Maroncita's arm, but she pulled away from his grasp.

99

"You cowboys!" she cried out. "You and your rough stock! You know how old my husband was when a saddle bronc fell on him in the arena and snuffed out his life? Twenty-two years old! We'd been married for all of eighty-seven days, six hours and thirteen minutes!"

chapter sixteen

When Lee got back to the chutes, King Richards had saddled one of the tryout horses himself and was ready to ride.

"Get the gate fer me, kid," he ordered. He climbed the chute gate as though he had done it much of his life, moving a bit stiffly, but with calm, cool concentration. He measured off his rein, slipped down into the saddle, found his stirrups, then nodded to Lee.

"Let's have 'im!" he drawled.

The big buckskin horse bolted out of the chute, stampeded a few yards to pick up speed, then went to bucking high and hard. Lee stared in amazement. Up to that point, Ruff Burleigh had been the best bronc rider he had ever seen. But King had a style and grace matched by no one else. He was balanced on a patch of saddle no bigger than a handkerchief, spurring with long, smooth strokes, taking chances, riding wild and reckless as though taking out his fury on himself.

When the horse had bucked far enough to be judged for quality, he waved aside the advancing pickup men as though he couldn't be bothered with them, stepped in his right stirrup, bent his left leg at the knee, sailed out into the air, and landed catlike on his feet, glancing off at the retreating bronc as though to further assess his talents from the ground.

Lee rode the next horse, a blue roan with a Roman nose and a back kick like a mule. The horse went plumb loco, turning back and bucking against the chutes, kicking at Lee's feet, biting at the stirrups, and squealing. When he finally straightened up, he went bucking across the arena, where he stumbled and fell. Lee lit rolling, barely escaping being crushed. The horse scrambled to his feet and stood, eyes rolling in terror, feet wide apart. When Lee moved to get up off the ground, the animal snorted and whirled away from him.

"Locoweed!" King Richards growled.

The owner of the horses, a fat, jolly man, had been sitting on the fence watching. King confronted him in two giant strides.

"Yuh got any more hosses in this herd been eatin' locoweed," he snapped, "yuh better git 'em outa the bunch pronto. Good way tuh kill a cowboy. Lookit thet last crazy cayuse. Run plumb intuh the fence down by the catch pens!"

King walked down the chutes, peering in at the animals, waving a gloved hand at each of them and watching their eyes. "What about this un?" he asked, nodding toward the animal in Chute Five.

The little fat man rubbed his hands together nervously. "He's a bucker, that one. Bought him at an all Indian rodeo in northern Nevada."

"Well, he's loco!" King said. "Scared of his own shadow."
He opened the gate, turning the horse out. The bronc went
running out ducking and dodging, spooking at every
shadow, its actions suspiciously uncoordinated.

"Whut about it?" King snapped. "Yuh got any more of
them zombies in here?"

"Skip the gray," the little man said. "He came off the same
range."

Lee came out on another big buckskin with a black stripe
down its back. There was nothing loco about that horse; he
was worth all the rest of them put together. High and wild,
a real crowd pleaser. Halfway out, he sucked back, caught
Lee napping, and left the boy hanging in midair. Lee lit on his
shoulder and bounced. For a moment, he propped himself on
his elbow and watched the horse, memorizing every jump,
making sure he knew what had gone wrong for next time.

King looked pleased with that one and watched him until
the animal disappeared into the catch pens. Then he climbed
the chute again and took the next bronc out.

The horse looked like someone's pet saddle horse, but he
was no green bronc. He turned inside out, but King floated
on him with grace, took every jump the horse could throw
at him, then stepped off again into midair. Lee thought he
saw the man wince with pain as he hit the ground on his feet;
but when he turned, the mask was back in place, and he was
as inscrutable as ever.

Maybe he's acting out a role, Lee thought, *playing the role
of the man he was once and the one he would like his son
Jimmy to be.*

There was one more sound horse to try. Lee threw his
saddle up on the chute, but King grabbed his own saddle as

103

it came back from the catch pens and moved to take Lee's turn. The older man was breathing a little hard and walked as though his kidneys hurt him. He started up the chute gate, then changed his mind, letting Lee have the horse. As Lee settled down on the animal's back, he looked across the arena and saw that the pre-rodeo bustle had begun. Scattered handfuls of spectators already lounged about the stands, and calf ropers, team ropers, and bulldoggers were all getting their horses loosened up for the day's run.

The pinto horse wasn't big, but he was fast and made Lee earn every penny. He tried his best to imitate King's long, smooth leg motions and almost lost the horse beneath him, then played it a bit more caustiously the rest of the ride. As he walked back, the crowd in the stands gave him a good hand. King Richards even managed a smile.

"Yuh are pretty quick to pick up another man's tricks, Lee," he said. "Wal, jus' remember yuh've got a pretty fair style all yore own."

Lee flushed with the compliment. King had actually called him Lee instead of kid and had been friendly to him! That meant a lot to his confidence.

On the way back to Maroncita's van, Lee passed Ruff Burleigh. Ruff's black hat rode low on his forehead, and he wore a pair of aviator's glasses; but the big, dark lenses did not quite hide the discoloration around one eye. He carried a bottle of beer in one hand, and from the way he walked, he might be a little drunk. As he walked, he looked from one face to another, as though spoiling for a fight.

He might have been champion once, Lee thought, *but he doesn't have a thing I want now.*

He detoured to keep out of Ruff's way and approached the van just as Maroncita returned from the hospital.

"He'll be all right," she said quietly. "Broken ribs and a slight concussion, but he's tough. I talked with him some. Says he'll never make another King Richards show. Wants to move to Oregon and maybe get into ranching."

Pam came out of King's van and stood listening to Maroncita. Lee could see she had been crying. He looked at her and smiled, then took up a curry comb, walked over to the mares, and went to cleaning them, rubbing them down with oil. He was aware that Pam stood watching him, but he did not turn.

"Lee," she said. "I don't know how to say this, but I—want you to be careful. I—don't want anything to happen to you."

He didn't know how to handle talk like that, so he just flashed her a smile and went on working. When he turned, finally, she was gone.

He grabbed a hamburger over at the concession stand. A girl who worked there gave him a big smile and tried to flirt with him. She looked around quickly to see if anyone was watching, then tried to give him the hamburger for free. He left the money on the counter anyway and went back to get the horses ready for the grand entry. Maroncita was all business, as though the pressures of the morning had never existed.

It wasn't Ruff Burleigh's day. In the calf roping, he made a good catch, but when he made his tie of three legs, the calf kicked out of the pigging string and got loose, disqualifying him. He made a good jump in the bulldogging, but the steer tripped and went down. He had to let the animal up and throw him again, which added seconds to his time. And in the saddle bronc riding, he drew Blackhawk—not the horse to come out of the chute on when you're nursing a hangover. Blackhawk went into a spin, and it was like dropping a marble on a spinning phonograph platter. Burleigh went hurtling up the chutes and landed on a pile of saddles.

Top Rail and Mastadon both bucked their riders off, and that left Lee under pressure. He had drawn Yellow Fever and was faced with the prospect of maybe getting into the money. *Maybe I ought to play it safe*, he thought, *and hope enough of the other contestants get bucked off to let me place.* But as he settled down on the big palomino, he saw King Richards out there in the arena watching and decided, win or lose, to try to make a good ride.

He came out of the chute spurring, and the big horse almost broke Lee's head open on the announcer's platform, then rattled his teeth as he jolted the ground in front of the chutes with all four feet. After a bad second or two when he thought Yellow Fever had bested him, Lee caught the rhythm and began to spur to impress the judges. Ten seconds flew by, and when the whistle blew, he was really hitting his stride.

He liked the sound of the applause and hoped the judges heard it, too. As he started back toward the chutes, he heard Mel Lambert at the microphone, giving him a little build-up. "It was only a couple of months ago, here in Montana, that I first watched young Lee Overalls trying out bucking horses for King Richards, and I want to tell you just how much that cowboy has improved. I'm going to come right out and say it publicly; if he keeps on improving, some day this youngster may end up Champion of the World!"

Lee looked up at the announcer above the chute and shook his head modestly, but he was pleased. The two judges had an option of scoring a ride from 65 to 85 points each, and he was glad to get a combined point total of 154 on the ride, putting him in the lead.

In the bull riding, he had drawn a big spotted bull named Thirteen. The bull was mostly brahma, but some Hereford ancestry had given him a white face and orange markings along his white flanks. Lee thought it was a bad draw. Thirteen was big and stout, and right now, after a long and vigorous day, there wasn't much stout left in his arm.

He had won the day before because so many bull riders had ended up on the ground. Today, four cowboys had managed to ride, and Lee knew if he wanted to end up in the money, he'd have to be spectacular. *This is the last bull I'm ever going to try,* he thought, *so I may as well give it all I've got.*

Thirteen was loose-hided, ugly-tempered, unpredictable, and bad news to most cowboys. And he was just as unpopular with the clowns, who earned their money every time he came charging out of the chute.

On the first jump, Thirteen whipped Lee over on his side, and it took lots out of his arm to straighten up. He kept slamming his boots against the bull's shoulders to right himself, and as if sensing he had the boy in trouble, the bull kept bucking harder and harder, slinging his massive head as though to sweep the rider off his back. His hide was so loose on his back, it seemed impossible to get a good leg hold on the body underneath.

Lee leaned back against his handhold, trying desperately to zig when the bull zigged, zag when he zagged. The bull spun to the left, then countered to the right, but still the boy clung to his back. When the whistle blew, Lee had had enough of that bull. He jerked his hand loose from the rigging and stepped off, as the enraged bull whirled and tried to catch him with his horns.

From the roar of the crowd, Lee knew he was in trouble.

The bull caught him in the ribs with a horn, and the boy saved himself by placing one hand on the animal's forehead and straight-arming himself away. The bull stopped dead in his tracks, shook his head angrily and began to stalk him with short, mincing steps.

The clown cut behind the bull trying to distract him, but the bull shook his head at the clown and kept on coming, inch by inch. Lee knew his best chance lay in trying to get the big animal moving and then trying to outmaneuver him. Sensing that the bull was about to explode, Lee acted first. He lurched suddenly forward, slapping the startled bull on the nose. As the bull dropped one horn and burst forward, Lee rolled away from the horn, drove hard past the bull's shoulder and hip, and kept going, just as the clown teamed up with him and came in from the other side to distract him.

As Lee gained the fence, he was so winded he didn't hear the announcer call out his score. He hadn't been bucked off, but he felt that he had done poorly. Though at least he had managed to right himself and finish the ride fairly strong.

The final bull rider came out and got dumped on his head.

Lee left the chute area exhausted. Vaguely he heard the announcer mention Lee Overalls, but it didn't seem to register. It was just a name they had given him in place of Lee Oliver Rawls, and right now he didn't seem to be anybody at all. He kept walking, thinking, cussing himself out for not making a better ride, wishing that he had the chance all over again.

Maroncita met him near the van, her face pale beneath her make-up.

"I don't know whether to hug you or feel sorry for you," she said with a thin smile.

He gave her a questioning look, wondering if she were

making fun of him. He could have done better on that bull; he hated failing.

The woman stared at him. "You don't even know how you came out?"

He shook his head.

The laugher came then in ringing peals. She leaned back against her van, her face wreathed in smiles.

"You're something else, Lee Overalls. Most of these cowboys have heads that will hardly fit their hats; you don't even know how good you are. Do you have any idea what you just won? For the whole show? First in saddle bronc riding, first in bull riding! And a big silver belt buckle for being best all-around cowboy in the rodeo!"

chapter seventeen

❖

That evening Lee and Maroncita went to see Jimmy in the hospital. The boy was under sedation for pain, but he recognized them immediately. He seemed happy that Maroncita was there, and not a little embarrassed to see Lee.

This was one of those times when not having to carry on a conversation was a relief. Lee sat in a chair, mellow with fatigue, marveling at how easily Maroncita filled the room with cheer. He was relieved that Jimmy did not ask how the rodeo came out. Instead, he fretted about his hospital bill. He hadn't saved much money, and of course, he would never again accept help from his dad.

Lee could understand Jimmy's fears. He too was alone, and if he got hurt riding broncs, there would be no one to go to bat for him and pay his bills.

He got up out of the chair and wandered down the hall.

When he returned a half hour later, Jimmy was asleep and Maroncita sat quietly by his side.

They had gained the hospital exit when Maroncita excused herself and left Lee waiting for a time in the waiting room. He thought perhaps she had gone to consult with Jimmy's nurses and did not give her absence another thought. When she came back out of the hospital, she gave Lee a curious glance, then slid into the driver's seat of the pickup she had borrowed from friends.

As they drove back towards the fairgrounds and the arena, she turned once as though to talk to him, then changed her mind.

By the time they had returned to the rodeo grounds, many of the contestants had moved on, heading to other rodeos. The camp lay asleep with only a few glimmerings of light. Lee saw Maroncita to her door and stood for a moment at her side. In the pale light her face seemed almost luminous. "Lee," she said, taking his big hand in hers. "Lee, that was a nice thing you did for Jimmy."

He looked at her as though he didn't know what she was talking about, and she smiled. "You see, while you were waiting for me at the hospital, I went back in to make arrangements to pay Jimmy's expenses. They told me something at the desk I hadn't expected. They said a tall young cowboy had just come down the hall not twenty minutes before and made arrangements to pay the bill. It'll take most of your winnings, Lee. You're going to have to let me share."

When King Richards pulled out of the rodeo grounds the next morning, bound for the next rodeo, he left Jimmy's Australian shepherd, Bum, behind. As though sensing he

111

had been abandoned, Bum came creeping over to Lee's rolled-up bedroll and stationed himself beside it.

"Look, Lee!" Maroncita said, touching his shoulder. "It looks as though you've got yourself a dog."

Realizing that he was under scrutiny, Bum crouched down and laid his nose on his paws, but remained alert to their every word and movement. He was a pretty animal, with long black hair, a white brisket, fawn markings on muzzle and brows, and more adoration in his eyes than a setter.

"Well, come on, Bum," Maroncita said when the horses were loaded, and it was time to depart. "You may as well ride!" Not having to be invited twice, the dog bounded from his bed, leaped into the back of the van, and settled in a manger.

As they passed through the heart of town, Maroncita parked at a shopping center to stock up with groceries. Left to his own devices, Lee looked through the Yellow Pages and located a medical center only three blocks away.

He felt pleased when Maroncita offered to go to the doctor with him. He helped her load her groceries, then, leaving the van parked in the shade of a giant cottonwood, they moved off together down the city streets.

Lee found that breaking old habits was hard. He walked along the streets feeling afraid to meet someone out of his past, checking every face in the crowd as though one of them would turn out to be Slick. When a policeman approached them just outside a school, he wanted to find an alleyway into which he could duck, but there was no running. With Maroncita along, all he could do was walk bravely forward.

I'm a fool, he thought. *The police don't want me in Montana. I haven't stolen anything here, and I'm not about to. I've gone straight, but it sure takes some getting used to!*

The doctor examined Lee's throat but could find nothing wrong. He smiled at Lee, then at Maroncita. "How long," he asked, "has the young man been without a voice?"

Maroncita turned to Lee for an answer. He took up a pen and wrote out honest answers to the doctor's questions. He hadn't noticed his voice leaving; it was just that after that bull ride, when Jimmy had first accused him before those other cowboys of being a thief, his voice had vanished. True, he'd suffered a blow from the bull's horn, but somehow he didn't think that was the real cause. But the fact remained that he was unable to make a sound.

"Sometimes," the doctor said, touching Lee's temple, "the injuries to one's body aren't all physical, and often a doctor can't do anything to help. If there is to be a healing, it has to come from within."

There was little Lee could do but accept this opinion. A series of one and two day rodeos followed. Lee got bucked off saddle broncs more often than he rode, but each trip out of the chutes was practice for him. On and on they went with all too little chance for rest. So both Lee and Maroncita were ready for some time off when she announced a break in their schedule.

"We've got five whole glorious days before the next rodeo," Maroncita gloated, "and only a couple of hundred miles to drive. I've always been in a hurry in my life, driving day and night to make my contract dates. But this year, thank goodness, I left a few gaps. I decided that life was too short, that I was going to run barefoot earlier in the spring and later in the fall, and enjoy life while I'm reasonably young."

During that five day respite, they stopped where they felt like it, soaking away bruises at hot spring resorts, catching trout for breakfast in small streams. Often they rode the horses back into the mountains, exploring the back country, panning for gold along the edges of the clear mountain streams. When Lee found a nugget, water-worn and polished to a high luster, they were like happy children and trooped up the canyon looking for the mother lode from which it came until they were breathless with exhaustion.

Camas flowers turned the high, moist meadows into blue lakes, and on the drier, rocky headlands, pasque flowers seemed far showier than anything Nature should allow. Exhilerated by the thin air, they raced each other for wild strawberries on the meadows, staining their fingers and lips scarlet as they picked.

Often they tied their horses securely to aspens or pines and climbed up over rocky battlements to sit and face the summer wind, perched like two old mated eagles on an eyrie, looking out over a vast kingdom. It was as though in each of their lifetimes, however different, neither of them had stopped running before and paused, simply to look, to wonder, and to enjoy.

When she's not performing in an arena, Lee thought, *she's different, and a lot more fun. But even now she's like an actress playing a part. But then, maybe I'm doing that myself. Playing at being a rodeo cowboy. Playing a role of being kind of—well—decent. Square. Which one is really me? This one or the role I played with Slick?*

Neither of them knew the names of the flowers and birds around them, so they made them up, Maroncita calling them out in her husky, vibrant voice, and Lee recording his inventions on paper.

"It's the beginning of the world," she called to him one

day from a rocky ledge well up the side of a mountain. "The great chief of our tribe has charged you and me with writing the first language!" She turned and ran quickly up a jumble of rocks to the very top, where she and Bum stood waiting patiently as Lee, struggling in the thin mountain air, came plodding along behind.

"Roag bamma ditsam!" he wrote on a piece of paper as they stood together on the lightning-scarred pinnacle overlooking the long, green valley of the Big Hole River.

"What on earth does that mean?" she asked gaily.

It means "I love you," he wrote in answer.

She laughed, gave him a hug, and kissed him shyly, but he saw a shadow pass over her face as though a broad-winged eagle had passed between them and the sun. Seconds later she was jogging down the hillsides, with Bum scampering at her heels, moving ahead now and then to chase a ground squirrel out of her path.

For a long time, he sat leaning against the rocks, feeling their welcome warmth, watching her diminish in size from woman to girl, to child, before she disappeared entirely into flatland forests. When Lee caught up with her again, she was already in the van fixing lunch. Coffee perked on the stove, and two mountain trout, which she had managed to catch in the adjacent brook, were doing slow contortions in the sizzling butter of the pan.

The next day was a travel day, but still they managed a short ride in the morning and a trip through a western museum that afternoon. The days had fled all too quickly, and they were reluctant to leave the hills and go to work again.

Lee was unloading the mares behind the arena when he

noticed a big blue Appaloosa horse tied to a trailer and heard a familiar, raspy voice boom out, "Hey, Lee Overalls! Where 'n hell hev yew been?"

He looked up to see Slim Pickens ambling his way, trailed by the usual retinue of kids. "Yew know whut, Lee?" he said. "Somebody I was talkin' tew told me yew hit quite a lick at one of those rodeos a few weeks back, winnin' the bronc ridin', the bull ridin', and the all-around. I told them, by golly, thet COULDN'T be the Lee I knew, 'cause he couldn't ride a stick horse if it was tied tew a fence." He grinned his famous grin. "He, he, he!" he chuckled.

Slim slapped Lee on the back, and the troupe following at his heels looked at the young cowboy with real envy.

Lee grinned, enjoying the attention. Slim had brightened his life considerably, but he held the friendship in proper perspective. Slim knew everyone, liked most of them, and made folks laugh whether he was doing it professionally or just off somewhere having a visit. Slim needed people around him, and you hardly ever saw him alone.

"By golly, Lee," Slim said. "I got another favor tew ask yew. Howja like tew work the barrel fer me again this show?"

Lee nodded, pleased to be asked. He had definitely made up his mind to rest on his laurels in the bull riding and concentrate on saddle broncs, so the barrel would present no problem.

The rodeo committee was giving a barbecue for contestants that evening, but Lee avoided going, choosing instead to spend the evening with the horses and the dog, Bum. His inability to talk to people made him especially shy. As he polished the horses to a high sheen and covered them with light nylon blankets against the night air, he could hear a country western band from over under the lights and the sound of people talking and laughing. He was feeling just a little sorry for himself when Pam and Maroncita came to get him and dragged him, one on each arm, to the big bash.

"You can't let yourself miss this, Lee," Pam scolded. "There are lots of top rodeo people here. Lindermans, Greenoughs, folks that have played a big part in rodeo history. They'll want to meet you. Everybody's talking about you as a real comer."

Lee didn't think of himself as much. He was wise enough to know that he'd been lucky. If some of the other cowboys hadn't had tough breaks, he might not have won. His scores hadn't been that high. But in rodeo, Lady Luck could be fickle. Sometimes, being at the right rodeo, at the right time, and drawing the right stock meant as much as talent.

Maroncita led him forward to a group of people who were sitting about on a ring of folding chairs, talking over old times.

"I want you to meet Marge and Alice Greenough," Maroncita said. "If you think you men are the only ones that can ride rough stock, Lee, you're badly mistaken. The Greenough girls thrilled crowds at Madison Square Garden and many another rodeo and were pretty darn hard to buck off."

Lee didn't know exactly where to look. All he could see in the throng before him were a couple of slender, well-dressed ladies, not the Amazons she was describing. But it was those very ladies who smiled at her introduction, put out their slender hands to shake his, and offered him punch from a bowl on the table.

"And this is their brother, Turk," Cita went on. "Turk, Lee Overalls." Lee smiled again, shaking hands with the tall, rugged cowboy.

117

"And all of you remember Pam Richards, of course," Maroncita went on.

"Tell us about your brother, Jimmy," Alice Greenough asked. "We heard he was in the hospital."

"He'll be all right," Pam said. "Jimmy'll be up and around in no time."

A press photographer came up as they were talking. "Maroncita, Alice, Marge," he said. "Mind if I take the three of you together? Having you girls in town is front page stuff."

"It's all right with me, Joe," Maroncita said. "But you'd better include Lee Overalls here. He may turn out to be the hottest thing in rodeo before the summer's out. And here's Pam Richards. She'll be a champion barrel racer some day."

Lee had a gut feeling that he didn't want his photograph taken for the newspapers, but Pam and Maroncita both mistook his hesitation for shyness and drew him into the picture.

"So this is Lee Overalls," the newsman said when he had taken the photograph. "I was looking for him. Slim Pickens told me about him, said I might get an interview. OK by you, Lee?"

Lee thought of his voice and the notoriety and shook his head.

"No interviews with our star," Pam Richards said firmly, taking the reporter by the arm. "But I'm available. I'm handling Mr. Overall's press. What is it you'd like to know?"

"That girl!" Maroncita laughed, and the other all smiled.

Pam seated the startled newsman off to one side on a bale of hay and proceeded to pour out a long account of Lee Overall's virtues as a clown, a rider of rough stock, and a man who just plain had a way with animals.

"And girls!" The reporter laughed.

"Lawsy me, no!" Pam protested.

The reporter tried to change the subject. He was hearing more about Lee than he really needed to know.

Alice Greenough laughed. "I think that young lady is rather smitten with you, Lee!"

Lee flushed, glancing quickly at Maroncita, but he was relieved that she had moved a little way off and was having an earnest conversation with Turk Greenough.

Lee began to wish he'd stayed with the horses. The thought of having his picture in newspapers worried him. He was in a quandary. If he handed the reporter a note asking him not to use his picture, the newsman might wonder if he had something to hide. And if it did go into the papers, there was the tiny but frightening chance that someone might recognize him, even Slick himself.

The fragrance of barbecued buffalo wafted over the crowd. Lee excused himself and went over to a table where some ladies were selling tickets for the supper. He bought tickets for Pam, Maroncita, and himself, and then an extra one for Bum. He waited patiently as a gray-haired lady at a typewriter pecked out name cards to go on their shirts. Lee wrote out each name separately on a slip of paper, then handed them to the woman.

"Lee Overalls!" the woman exclaimed. "I feel as though I know you. I watched you ride last week, up north!"

Lee delivered the badges to the girls, and together they stood in line, helping themselves from tables heaped with food. The local women had tried to outdo each other in giving a bash to make the rodeo folk welcome. Lee had never dreamed such food existed.

"Oh, oh!" Maroncita exclaimed to Pam. "From the way Lee's trying everything, I have a feeling I'm in trouble. He'll

119

expect me to cook like this. Up to now he's been patient. Sunday dinner has been hamburger with cheese."

The buffalo meat was delicious. Sitting between Maroncita and Pam, surrounded by rodeo folk who seemed to accept him, Lee thought he had never been happier.

As he ate sitting on bales of hay, he glanced about him, reading name tags on other contestants. Bill McMacken, Doff Aber, Orrie Dooley, Jack Spurling, Carl Shepherd, John Bowman, Gene Rambo, Stub Bartlemay, Bill Linderman. On bales next to Pam, three bronc riders, Ken Madland, Ross Dollarhide, and Cecil Henley, were talking saddle broncs.

"That old Sceneshifter." Henley laughed. "Sometimes old Shifter would throw his head around and look right at yuh." The man's affection for the great old bucking horse came through.

"How long you been at this game, Cece?" Ross asked.

"Well, sir," Henley said. "I've been ridin' saddle broncs for twenty-seven years!"

Across the way, Mel Lambert and Slim Pickens were trading yarns. Gathered around them, enraptured by their stories, were a dozen other big name cowboys. Lee felt suddenly intimidated. He'd been lucky those last rodeos. Much of the heavy talent had been contesting further south. Well, he'd do the best he could. This rodeo was going to be a good learning experience for him. He planned to watch every one of these cowboys carefully, figuring out their styles and how they got the best out of each horse. When they out-scored him, he would try to figure out why.

That evening, he left early to check Maroncita's horses, so that she could stay and enjoy herself. Pam asked if she could come along, but he shook his head.

Pam was all right, and he liked her as a friend. It was just that, well, he felt so close to Maroncita. He didn't quite know how to handle this thing with Pam, how to keep her at a distance without hurting her feelings.

As he walked across the lot behind the stock pens, with Jimmy's dog, Bum, trotting along behind, he passed King Richards, working all alone to get the stock ready for morning.

King glanced at him as he passed, but if he recognized him or saw Jimmy's dog trotting at his heels, he gave no sign. The boy was about to stop and offer the older man a hand, but King turned from him and disappeared into the gloom beyond the world of lights.

chapter eighteen

uff Burleigh's bay quarter horse mare woke Lee at dawn. She had worked herself loose and, dragging her tie rope, had come across the way to where he slept and stood nuzzling his ear. Lee reached up and scratched the white star on her face. She was Ruff's bread and butter, that mare, hard-working, fast and sensible. Burleigh used her himself, but also lent her out to other doggers, claiming a share of their winnings. At any particular rodeo, she might come out of the box four or five times a performance.

Lee got up out of his bedroll, dressed, and led the mare back to where she had been tied. Through the thin walls of the trailer, he heard the low gutteral snoring stop, then the dry, hacking cough of a heavy smoker, as the cowboy woke up. He tied the mare quickly and got out of there, knowing Burleigh would be quick to assume he was stealing the horse instead of bringing her back.

It was too late to go back to sleep. He wandered over to the stock corrals, climbed in with the horses and visited with them. Blackhawk came over and nosed his pocket as though remembering that the last time he had done that an apple had appeared.

The big black's coat was beginning to shine. King took good care of his horses, graining them morning and evening. With Jimmy gone, and the old man Bart Shelley off settling his affairs, King tended the stock himself, as though afraid a hired man might give an animal too much grain and founder him.

Lee's friends among the saddle broncs surrounded him, pushing up against him for their share of attention. He rubbed Blackhawk's nose, then moved to his shoulder and patted him along his long back and hips. Lee glanced out over the corral fence, but could see no one stirring. Taking a mane hold, he eased himself up on the huge animal. The heavy muscles tensed beneath him, as the horse humped up and clamped his tail tightly to his body. Then the horse looked around at him, nipped at him as though to let Lee know he was taking his chances, then relaxed, a soft, contented look returning to his dark eyes.

One, two, three, four, five, six, seven, eight, nine, TEN! Lee counted to himself. *There's the whistle! Friend Eddy*, he mused, *there's a great saddle bronc named Blackhawk, which some rodeo folk say is as great as one of the most famous broncs of all time, Five Minutes Till Midnight. Blackhawk has bucked everybody off so far. Well, guess where I am now, Eddy. I'm sitting on his back. Course he's just standing here in the corral. Out of a chute, he'd buck me off quick as a flash. You might say I'm building up my confidence for some day when I get him in the draw.*

He heard a truck start up and slipped off the big horse just in time. When King Richards and Pam drove up, he had taken a pitch fork and was putting fresh hay in the mangers.

King took a sack of grain, set it on the tailgate of the pickup truck, then took a gallon can and began to measure oats into some burlap nose bags.

"Ef yuh don't mind givin' me a hand," he said, "slip a nose bag on each o' these broncs fer me."

He shook his head as Lee wandered at will among the animals, coaxing each animal to turn and face him as he draped a nose bag over each muzzle and up over their ears.

"Dad," Pam asked. "Wasn't Bart Shelley supposed to come back after his wife's funeral and take care of Blackhawk and the rest of the broncs for you?"

"I reckon thet's whut he promised," King said sadly. "But I hed a hunch the old feller'd made other plans. Losin' his ranch, his wife, an' havin' tuh part with Blackhawk—it was all too much fer him. I should'a known he'd take mah offer tuh pay the funeral expenses as charity. He was some proud, thet ol' man. He sent me a bill of sale fer Blackhawk. The next morning someone found him dead. 'Natural causes,' the Doc said. My guess is he died of a broken heart."

King moved off down the corral fence to tend to the brahma bulls, as though he just didn't want to talk anymore, and Pam followed after to give him a hand.

He looks ten years older this morning, Lee thought, noting the stiffness in King's gait. *I can't believe that not long ago I saw him riding broncs like a young man.*

He took the feed bags off the horses and draped them on a bale of hay just across the fence, then headed back toward the van.

As he left the pens, Ruff Burleigh came out of his trailer,

his massive, black-haired chest bare, hair frowsy with sleep. He scratched himself like an ape, crossing his muscular arms across his chest, then did a few desultory exercises, which seemed more from force of habit than from any real desire to keep in shape. His shoulders were still powerful, but beer had given him the start of a paunch. As Lee passed, Ruff glanced over, then dismissed him as being unworthy of even a nod.

There were other stirrings around the encampment. Across from Maroncita's, a cowboy, also naked to the waist, his hands and face below the hatline bronzed by wind and sun, the rest white as milk, came out of a trailer, yawned, inspected the sky for weather, took a pile of hemp and a steaming cup of coffee, sat down on a bale, and proceeded to braid away on a new bull rope. A pickup truck with Texas plates, towing a four horse trailer, drove onto the grounds, and three cowboys piled out, stiff and bleary-eyed, as though they had driven all night.

As he curried Maroncita's animals, Lee looked off over their backs, watching the scene unfold and begin to bustle with activity. He was aware suddenly of how he was coming to enjoy this life and feel very much a part of it. Nevertheless, he was depressed over the news about Bart Shelley; and once the horses were done, he jogged along behind some other cowboys around the race track, finishing off with a strenuous set of exercises designed to improve his strength. He had finished a shower in the improvised canvas stall provided by the rodeo committee and dressed, when Maroncita called him in for breakfast.

That afternoon, on a whim, he tried his first bareback bronc, a little bald-faced black, with one blue eye and white stockings. He rosined his glove, took the single leather handle of a Pete Dixon bareback rigging with what felt like a grip of iron, settled down on his back, and nodded to the gate man. The first jump, he leaned back and tried to spur the animal the way he'd seen others do it, but he missed the rhythm, and the quick little animal dumped him on his head.

"Oh, my!" the announcer groaned. "Well, he was makin' a good ride until some darned fool opened the gate and let him out!"

Slim Pickens gave him a hand up off the ground and dusted him off.

"Yew know whut, Lee," he grinned. "I think yew better stick tew saddle broncs."

In the first section of the saddle bronc riding, Ruff Burleigh came out on a stout, fast-kicking roan horse named Blue Blazes and, cigarette dangling from his lip, made a cold, calculated ride. But one of the judges claimed Burleigh touched the animal with his free hand and disqualified him. Burleigh's face turned brick red, and a hush fell over the cowboys along the fence as the big, mean cowboy glared at the judge and stalked back to the chutes.

It was another bad day for Burleigh. Lee was helping out over at the calf chutes, restretching the rubber inner tube barrier after each run, when Ruff hurtled out of the box on a borrowed sorrel rope horse, chasing a black droop-eared calf. Still upset about disqualifying in the bronc riding, he missed his calf completely. The crowd, who had taken a dislike to him, laughed aloud.

Refusing the second loop to which he was entitled, Ruff rode back to the calf chutes, coiling his rope as he rode. The young horse he was riding spotted some other horses and nickered to them.

"Shut up, you hammerhead!" Burleigh roared, jerking on

the reins. In a frenzy, he whipped the animal over and under with his loop.

Never having seen such cruelty before, Lee stared in amazement. Frightened and confused, the sorrel began to prance, and throwing his head, knocked the big man's hat off. Burleigh beat on him again for that.

"Cut that out, Ruff!" Slim called. "Simmer down!"

You! Burleigh! Lee thought, mouthing the words, trying desperately to shout.

Ignoring the fact that the cowboy outweighed him by fifty pounds, Lee leaped from the fence, caught the startled cowboy by the shoulders, and carried him to the ground. Ruff boiled up first and was on his feet before Lee could get to his knees. The boy never saw the blow coming. There was a flash of light as Burleigh's fist caught him along the jaw.

When he came to, Slim was tending him behind the roping area. "Well!" Slim grinned. "Yew shore got yerself in a peck of trouble thet time." His big hand gripped Lee's shoulder. "Yew know whut? Yew done the right thing, even if it wasn't the smartest move anyone ever made."

Lee grinned shyly, moving his jaw to make sure it wasn't broken. He glanced at Slim and thought, *If I ever again catch Burleigh mistreating a horse, I'll fight him, just like today!* He pulled himself to his feet, refusing Slim's hand.

For a few minutes he sat on a fence watching the barrel racers compete and joined the applause as Pam made a spectacular run. Then, suddenly, there was Ruff again, getting ready to make his bull dogging run. Lee pursed his lips and found out he could still whistle, in spite of Ruff's blow.

Just as Burleigh came galloping out, his little mare pounding hard to overtake the steer, Lee whistled like a wild stallion nickering for mares.

127

The bay mare lost her concentration, and just as Ruff leaped, the mare veered sharply away, leaving him hanging in midair. He missed his steer completely and skidded along in the dirt on his nose.

"Why, yew son of a gun!" Slim laughed. "Let me tell yew somethin', Lee. Yew got thet mare plumb in love!"

Burleigh limped up to his mare as she searched the fence for Lee. He took the reins over her ears and led her away, glaring up at Lee as he passed by. Lee stared back innocently, but it was apparent that Ruff had a good idea what had transpired.

"Yew know whut, Lee," Slim said, smiling, "I don't think thet cowboy cares fer yew." He climbed up beside the boy on the fence. "Seriously, kid," he said. "Ain't none of us cowboys envy yew now. Ruff Burleigh don't fergit easy. One day yew might jes' hev tew fight 'im, an' my advice tew yew would be tew start right now, gettin' yoreself in darn good physical shape."

chapter nineteen

ee was out of his league in the saddle bronc riding, and he knew it; but just competing against those big name cowboys was worth every penny of the entrance fees. Ross Dollarhide, the big, quiet, handsome young cowboy from Oregon, had been on a roll this season and was way out in front nationally in terms of dollars won. Barring injury, he seemed set to be the new world champion. Ross drew War Paint, who hadn't bucked very hard a week ago; but Ross made him look like one of the greats. Yet he himself was in control all the way.

Except for one or two cowboys like Lee, the rest were veterans who hadn't paid their entrance fees to buck off. Up to Lee's turn to ride, only Blackhawk and Yellow Fever had managed to buck off their riders. Lee settled down on Top Rail knowing he was just donating his entrance fees, but determined to make a good showing as far as he went.

"Hell, there's no point in ridin' 'im careful, Lee," Slim advised as he belted him down on the horse. "Let me tell yew somethin! Fergit about buckin' off. Fer as far as yew c'n go, shake these judges up with a wild ride they'll remember. It's a whole lot better to buck off spurrin' up a storm than to try to steal a ride. An' like old Harry Rowell, who had a buckin' string in California, told me once, 'Fifth place don't buy no groceries!'"

Lee had learned a few tricks that afternoon watching how Ross Dollarhide and Bill Linderman brought out the best in their horses. He came out of the chute feeding the little horse all the rein he could spare, riding him hungry, and the little horse bucked wild and chased both judges to the fence, then came back down the chutes scattering cowboys. By the time the whistle blew, Lee was feeling that there wasn't a bronc on this earth he couldn't ride. He ended up tied for fourth place; but most of all, he had proved that winning the all-around back along the trail hadn't been a fluke.

As he headed back toward the chutes, unbuckling his chaps as he walked, Ross Dollarhide gave him a big, shy grin and shook his hand. Pam was sitting on the gate when he left the arena. As he swung her around, she pulled off his stetson, kissed him atop his head, and replaced his hat. He grinned back at her, but he kept walking, looking for Maroncita, knowing she wasn't watching, but hoping at least that she'd heard the announcer.

She was busy in her van, however. She answered his knock and called for him to enter. He found her sitting at her vanity applying makeup. She smiled to acknowledge his presence, then frowned as she saw the bruise along his jaw where Ruff Burleigh had hit him. He wished he could talk to her about his day and casually let it slip about being tied for fourth place. Considering the competition, he was prouder of that feat than of winning back along the line. But she'd learn it from someone else before the day was out. Like it or not, he knew he'd be the subject of plenty of conversation. Better get back to work now.

He turned to leave, but she blocked the door.

"You're going to stay right here while I bathe that bruise on your jaw," she said. She heated a pan of boric acid on the stove and bathed the abrasion carefully.

"That hurt?" she asked.

He shook his head, wondering if she had heard how he'd gotten that bruise.

"Well, it's a long way from your heart," she said. She pushed him toward the door. "Get out of here now. I've got to get ready to ride."

As he led her horses to the track, she caught up with him and walked by his side. He moved on as though he didn't know she was in the world, wanting desperately every step of the way to tell her how beautiful she looked.

Perhaps she too had picked up inspiration from the great performers who thronged this rodeo. She waved to the Greenough girls, who were sitting with some of the officials in a box seat, then proceeded to bring the crowd to their feet with a spectacular series of rides.

"She worries about me riding rough stock," Lee thought, "when I'd be scared to death doing some of those suicide stunts she does!"

"Peanuts! Popcorn! Popcorn! Peatnuts! Get 'em while they're hot!"

Lee froze in his tracks. That voice! It was right out of his past. Could it be Slick? He looked up into the stands. A vendor's uniform had been one of Slick's favorite disguises!

There were several vendors working the crowd, and all of them in some way resembled Slick.

"Peanuts! Popcorn!" The voice again!

The vendor who had called was halfway up an aisle, reaching out to a customer to deliver a bag and pick up change. If it was Slick, he'd lost a little weight in jail.

"Peanuts! Popcorn!" The man was climbing away from him now, and Lee couldn't tell much.

But his blood was running cold. Slick had used that cover so often to work his trade, using that tray of bags to deliver contraband, or gather the contents of stolen wallets and smuggle them safely to a parked car somewhere, where the cash and anything else of value could be sifted out and the rest discarded. It was also a place to launder hot money or counterfeit bills.

It was all so simple. You could be sitting at a ball game right next to a cop and take delivery. Buy two bags, slip one into your pocket, and eat the contents of the other, even offering some to your neighbor, just to be friendly. A vendor could move at will in the crowd. Like apple pie, ice cream, hot dogs—an institution. Once the transaction was complete, the vendor's face was forgotten. There might be anything in those bags. Cocaine. Pot. A gun. Or peanuts laced with cyanide to take care of an informer.

"Peanuts! Popcorn! Last time around!" Another vendor, and he sounded like Slick, too. Maybe all vendors came to sound alike. Lee relaxed a little. As he busied himself with Maroncita's horses, he lost sight of the white-uniformed men in the stands. But when he glanced back and counted them, one of the men had disappeared. No need to panic; maybe he had sold out and gone for more.

But if it really was Slick working this crowd way up here

132

in Montana, then it wasn't a matter of chance. Slick had to be after him! He couldn't possibly have seen the photograph of him with Maroncita and the Greenoughs. There wasn't time. But maybe at Billings or any one of several other rodeos, when he hadn't been aware of a photographer—

He led Maroncita's mares back to the van, then changed into his clown outfit, the baggy pants, red suspenders, striped shirt, and derby hat Slim had provided. He smeared on the white grease paint and gave himself cherry lips and a strawberry nose. Slick wouldn't recognise him as a clown. Now he could work his way up into the stands and take a good look.

The second section of the barrel racing was on. As he moved into the arena, a pretty blonde girl, slender as a willow, lost her big hat as she streaked for the finish line. She rode out to pick it up, and Lee played the gentleman, dusted it off, and held it out to her. Just as she reached for it, however, he dropped it back on the ground, and the crowd laughed.

He blew a kiss to the audience, then climbed the fence and joined them in the grandstand, sitting himself down in one of the boxes, beside a pretty girl. He applauded loudly as Pam made her run and swept across the finish line in incredible time. Not realizing that he could not talk, the girl next to him asked him a question, but he smiled sadly, pointed to his Adam's apple, and was silent.

Leaving his seat, he climbed the steep stairs into the audience. One by one, he trapped the vendors and checked them out. Up close they didn't look anything like Slick. But there was one missing. What about him?

By now there were twenty children tagging along behind him, and he could hear the clang of cowbells along the chutes indicating the bull riders were getting set. He climbed down over the edge of the grandstand and crossed the track.

"Good-bye, Mister Overalls," a little girl called. He turned and smiled at her, then blew her a kiss.

Slim had barely rolled out the barrel for him, when, bell clanging, a ghostly gray brahma plunged out of the chutes, bucked off the rider in three waspy jumps, hesitated a split second as though deciding whether or not to hook the prostrate rider, then charged Slim instead, boiling through his cape like a freight train. Head high, hunting trouble, he spotted Lee and charged. Lee vaulted into the barrel and ducked inside, grabbing for his handholds. The bull hit the barrel a resounding whump and sent it flying, then followed it up, rolling the barrel across the arena with his horns until it smacked into the fence in front of the grandstand.

As the bull slid to a stop and stood shaking his horns, Slim rolled the barrel away from the fence, stood it back on end and looked in. "Yew okay, pardner?" he asked.

Lee nodded.

"This ole bull's as good a barrel bull as we've got. I'll play him some more. Hang on!"

Slim draped his cape across the barrel and teased the animal into a charge. But the bull was smarter now. He hit the barrel a short chopping blow, knocked the barrel over and tried to reach Lee through the open ends with his horns. Slim dashed in to turn the open ends away from him, then righted the barrel.

"He's watchin' us," Slim directed. "Pop out an' hit him in the face with yore hat!"

Lee put his head out; the bull was only three feet away. He sailed his hat, hitting the animal between the eyes, then dropped as the bull charged. Lee tried to duck, but missed his chance as the bull hooked the barrel. The boy's cheek smacked the wooden staves. The sound echoed through his head, and he felt the hot spurt of blood from his nostrils. He couldn't seem to get his legs tucked up.

The bull struck again, and Lee lost his grip on the cables. As the huge animal sent the barrel careening end over end, Slim kept running alongside, straightening the barrel when he could, trying to shove Lee back in. But the more he pushed on one end, the more of Lee came out the other.

"Suck it in, boy. Suck it in!" he shouted.

Sensing that his barrel man was a bit groggy, Slim ducked around the barrel to lead the bull away. Once Lee had risked his neck to save him and now was the time for repayment. Slapping the bull in the face, Slim took the charge and tried to cut away. As the crowd screamed, the bull caught the big cowboy between his horns and tossed him high.

Lee heard the awful roar of the crowd and knew that something had happened to Slim. He scrambled from the barrel just in time to see the bull catch the big man as he fell and toss him high again. Lee was shaky, but there was no fear in his bones. His one thought was to take the bull away.

He leaped over the barrel and caught the bull around the horns. The startled bull moved backwards one step, then another, dragging the boy, as Slim lit and scrambled away. The Ghost shook his horns, lifting Lee's feet off the ground, but still the boy clung to the animal's neck. He got one foot beneath him, then the other, then ducked away. As the bull lowered his head to catch him, Lee whirled and charged the bull, stepped between his horns, sailed over his back and landed on his feet. There was silence from the crowd for a moment, as though they were unsure of what they had seen. And then the applause started, scattered and uncertain at first, then thunderous, shaking the stands. The bull flung up his head as though not knowing quite where the boy had gone, then backed up a few steps, pawing nervously. As Slim rose to his knees and picked his fallen cape from the ground, the bull turned away and trotted off to the catch pens.

There wasn't time for much before the next bull was upon them, only a quiet glance between two friends who had gone through hell together.

That evening, there was a big rodeo dance, and Lee tried to beg off going, writing on a slip of paper that he had taken punishment enough for one day; but Pam and Maroncita only laughed and dragged him along between them. It wasn't the bruises really that mattered; after that scare with the popcorn vendors, he just wanted to keep away from public gatherings. He walked into the dance with Maroncita on one arm and Pam on the other, knowing that he must be the envy of every man in the room, but wishing he could just melt into the shadows. His glance worked every face in the crowd, looking for Slick.

It was then he realized that he had grown up, that he wasn't afraid of Slick any more. What he dreaded was that Slick would bring his new world crashing down around his head, and the role he was playing now with such success would suddenly end.

One by one, the greats of the rodeo world came up to shake his hand: Turk Greenough, congratulating him on his bronc ride; Leo Cramer, the famous rodeo livestock contractor and U.S. Senator; Jerry Ambler; Jack Sherman; Ross Dollarhide; and that famous old rodeo clown Homer Holcomb. Folks clustered around Pam too, excited about her time in the barrel racing. Pam flushed with the attention, and for the first time, Lee noticed how pretty she was. He soon forgot his fears. He had a real sense now of belonging to this world; these people were his friends.

He screwed up his courage, took Maroncita by the arm and led her toward the dance floor, feeling suddenly as frightened as he had been coming out on his first bull. She blushed like a young girl and held back, then just as quickly, as though sensing his disappointment, took his hand and led him out on the dance floor, as Pam watched them go.

Friend Eddy, he mused. *I'm sure in some kind of jam to-night. I came here with two girls, dumb old me, one on each arm, and unless I'm mistaken, Eddy, both of them are in love with me!*

He couldn't believe how easy it was. The way she led him, it was as though he'd been dancing for years. Once or twice he walked on her toes, then stopped and grinned at her before starting all over. He was painfully conscious of the warmth of her body and her firm, athletic waist.

He had never been so happy. He looked about the room and seemed to melt with warmth toward these people. They were his friends! They respected him for what he had learned to do! He glanced shyly down at Maroncita. He would die for her. If she needed it, he'd give her his last kidney. He couldn't even talk to these people, yet no one seemed to care.

He was leading Maroncita off the dance floor when he saw King Richards come in the door. His rugged features turned to granite as he saw Lee. He strode directly to Pam, spoke to her in a low voice, and they both turned to look at him, Pam's face a study of anguish.

Lee had no idea what was wrong, but his world crumbled beneath him as he headed their way. Pam glared at her father, matching his anger with her own. "Lee wouldn't do

137

something like that," she protested. "I just know he wouldn't!"

"What's wrong?" Maroncita asked.

"You come outside with me, boy," King snapped, ignoring her question.

There were two policemen waiting outside the door. They pushed Lee up against the wall and frisked him, taking away his pocket knife.

"What's going on here?" Maroncita demanded, moving to Lee's side and taking his arm.

One of the policemen looked at King Richards, then back at her. "There's been a burglary, ma'am. Mr. Richards lost a valuable silver-mounted saddle and a lot of valuable tack. He claims this boy did it."

The second policeman began reading Lee his rights.

"Just one minute," Maroncita said. "When did this theft take place?"

"Sometime after the last performance and just before the dance started," King said.

"There wasn't fifteen minutes of that time when Lee wasn't with me. You've no right to accuse him!"

"I told yuh when yuh hired 'im, he was a known thief," Richards growled. "Maybe he was with yuh when the theft took place, but sure as hell he set up the heist and his confederates moved in and took the goods!"

Slim Pickens came out of the door and stood listening. "I don't know whut the trouble is, Officer," he said, "but I'll vouch for Lee any day."

"You can't hold him just because Mr. Richards suspects him," Maroncita pleaded. "Lee works for me. I just know he wouldn't steal."

The officer in charge looked undecided.

"Look, Officer," Slim said. "I'll be responsible fer him stickin' around where yew can find him."

"I want him arrested right here an' now," King Richards said angrily.

"Sorry, Mr. Richards," the officer said weakening. "You see, we just don't have the kind of hard evidence we need to hold him." He glanced at Lee. "You stick around the grounds, young man. We may want to ask you some more questions."

When the officers had followed King Richards into the darkness, Slim put his hand on Lee's shoulder.

"Lemme put it to yew straight, Lee," he said. "Did yew hev anythin' to do with thet theft?"

Lee shook his head.

"Then all of us cowboys will dang sure stick by yew," Slim said.

Still in shock, Lee moved off into the darkness toward the van, and Maroncita followed him. His mind raced with possibilities. Maybe that had been Slick up in the stands. While everyone was at the dance, it would have been simple for him to move in, load King Richards' silver into a pickup, and scram. He didn't know quite what to do; if he told them about Slick, then the whole story of his previous life would have to come out too, and his fresh start would be wiped out.

"Lee!" Maroncita whispered as they approached her van. "Look!" The door had been wrenched violently from its hinges! The inside of the van was a shambles, and Maroncita's beautiful collection of silver, porcelain, and bronze was gone!

Maroncita bristled with anger and strode across the floor. Lee took her by the arm gently and held her back. There just ahead of her lay poor old Bum. He had tried to defend against the intruders and paid the price.

139

Maroncita laid her head against the boy's shoulder, then looked up at him. "You didn't do this, Lee. I know you didn't. Maybe before you came to me, you weren't always honest, but I know you'd never hurt an animal. I guess we'll have to go to the police with this, and I want you to know that, like your friend Slim, I'll stick with you all the way."

chapter twenty

Lee had a hard time going to sleep. He lay in his bedroll, staring up at the sky, trying to sort out what had happened. Maybe he was reaching out for something he wasn't meant to have. Maybe his mother had been wiser than he when she quit trying.

He heard the scrunch of boots walking on gravel, slow, tired steps, as someone moved through the sleeping encampment. He raised himself on one elbow and tried to pick out the person in the gloom, but the few all-night lights left on were over by the stands. He decided it was probably King Richards checking out his bucking horses before turning in. An eternity later, he heard the boots come scrunching back. The door to King's trailer opened, light stabbed the darkness, the door clicked shut, a lock snapped, and the jack-o-lantern face of the trailer went out as though the candle inside had been snuffed.

He fell into a fitful sleep and dreamed about Slick. He spotted his stepfather selling peanuts in the audience, leaped over the rail into the stands and, revolver drawn, pursued him. Carrying his tray supported by shoulder straps, the man moved higher and higher into the stands. Everywhere children clustered around the vendor, and he couldn't risk a shot. When he finally cornered the figure at the top of the grandstand, it turned to face him, and it was a little boy. "Peanuts! Popcorn! Mister! Last chance today!"

He shouted at the child. "I know who you are, and you're a thief! You're really Slick in disguise!"

"Lee! Lee! Stop screaming! You'll wake the whole camp!" It was Maroncita in her dressing gown. "You scared me," she said. "I heard voices and it was you, Lee, shouting and screaming in your sleep. Lee! You really have a voice after all!"

He tried to answer her, but the words wouldn't come.

"Lee," she said softly. "I'm scared, and I can't sleep. Maybe I shouldn't be saying this to you, but I want you to come and sleep indoors!"

He reached out and took her hand. For all the strong things it did during the day, it lay now in his hand like a crumpled bird. He put it to his cheek, then to his lips and kissed it.

Maroncita's bed was soft and gentle. He had been talking aloud in his sleep and sensed somehow that the barriers that had kept him silent were dropping away. He raised up on one elbow and looked at her face in the soft orange light of the guttering candle. If he could talk in his sleep, maybe now was the time to talk awake!

He could feel the words begin to form in his head, and the

142

vocal chords begin to respond. A sudden resonance was born again in his throat. It was like the strings of a dusty lute, standing mute and forgotten in the attic of an old house until discovered and touched by an exploring child.

"Roag bamma ditsam," he said aloud. "I love you!"

chapter twenty-one

Early the next morning, Lee buried poor old Bum down behind the bucking chutes. *If only the old dog could speak*, Lee thought, *he could tell us who did all this.*

Whoever it was that had entered Cita's van had been a stranger. Bum was friendly to everyone he knew. Except Jimmy, of course. He remembered the time that Bum had strayed over to Cita's van, and Jimmy had come to get him back. Bum had bitten the boy right through his glove. He wondered where Jimmy was now. Off doing anything but ride rough stock. King Richards had made a big mistake forcing his son to ride scared. It had been King's dream to have Jimmy follow in his footsteps, and now that dream would never happen.

The police were coming soon to inspect Maroncita's van, and he didn't want to be there. So he moved out onto the track to do his jogging. The cowboys in best shape suffered the fewest injuries.

Ordinarily, he quit after a couple of fast laps, but today he planned to keep going. The jogging would keep his mind off his troubles, and besides, he wanted to get into top shape in case Ruff Burleigh decided to pick a fight.

A pair of calf ropers finished jogging and dropped off the racetrack near their campers.

"Morning," Lee said, pleased that he still had a voice.

He began to run. The soft track felt good beneath his feet. A meadowlark sang from a corral fence, and he pounded steadily along, feeling the sweat begin to trickle from his brow and down between his shoulder blades, flowing clean and fresh from his pores. He was a wild stallion loping ever onward over vast sagebrush plains unmarred by fences or human campfires. He was Blackhawk, the great old outlaw who had never been tamed.

Far ahead of him on the track he saw a cowboy exercising his horse, coming his way, and as Lee jogged toward him, he recognised Ruff Burleigh. The man ignored him as he rode by, but the mare nickered to him. Burleigh booted her on with heavy heels.

Three more laps followed as Burleigh sat in the shade of his horse, leaning against the grandstand and watched him pass. It was on the fifth lap that Lee realized he had fallen into a trap. He could see Burleigh at a distance riding out on the track again, now trotting a little, now slowing to a walk, as though timing himself so that when he passed Lee, he would be at that point of the track furthest from the grandstand and screened from the encampment by a windbreak of Russian olive trees.

It was to have been his last lap, and the pace had been faster than he was used to. He ran with his mind blank, as though afraid he might think about being tired and collapse in a heap. He wished someone else would come out on the track, but the regulars had done their running and gone to the showers many minutes before.

He glanced back over his shoulder. A half mile away, he could see Cita and Pam exercising their horses together, behind the van. Ahead of him Burleigh dismounted, draped his reins over the inside rail of the track, then leaned insolently against the mare's hip, cigarette dangling from his lip, waiting for his approach.

"Well, boy," Burleigh said. "Someone told me yuh was trainin' tuh whip me. I guess yuh've run fur enough. I reckon now's the time to teach yuh a lesson yuh won't fergit!"

Lee's lungs hurt and his breath came in great gulps. He knew Burleigh's kind of fighter. They came in quick, caught their opponent by surprise, and punched them out. Usually they never needed a second blow. Lee thought his only chance lay in treating the big cowboy like a brahma bull, goading him to charge, then taking advantage of his motion.

He stood facing Burleigh, stealing all the breath he could. Burleigh took a step forward and stood firm.

If he were a bull he'd be pawing dirt, Lee thought. *He's fixing to charge.*

The words came out easily this time, crisp and clear. "You're yellow, Burleigh! You'll fight a horse, but you won't fight a man!"

With a bellow of rage, Burleigh leaped forward and threw a wild punch.

Lee stood calm, then sidestepped just as though he were handling a brahma bull. As the big cowboy hurtled past him,

146

Lee turned into the man, brought up his knee hard, and caught the older cowboy full in the paunch.

Burleigh bounced back, wary now, eyeing his opponent with new respect.

I'm dead right about him, Lee thought. *He's missed that first big haymaker, and now he doesn't quite know what to do.* He used that moment of indecision to suck a few more quarts of air into his lungs.

"You're a has-been, Burleigh! Look at that gut you're packing! The only good saddle bronc rides you make anymore are on a barstool somewhere!" It felt so good to talk, Lee hated to quit!

Burleigh winced and exploded into action. His big fist whistled past the boy's ear as Lee ducked, letting the force of the big man's blow carry him on past. The youngster caught him alongside the ear with a vicious chop. Burleigh was the barroom fighter relying on brawn; Lee was the street fighter whose survival had depended on knowing every dirty trick in the book.

Tied to the fence directly behind the man, the little bay mare was scared to death. She swung her rear end about just as Burleigh stepped back to duck Lee's blow and caught him full in the back with one hind quarter. The big cowboy went flying forward just as Lee connected with his nose.

The man fell heavily, and every time he tried to rise, Lee caught him with his boot and sent him sprawling again.

When Burleigh finally gave up and lay still, Lee walked up to the bay mare and quieted her by stroking her neck. After throwing the left stirrup leather up over her back, he unbuckled the buckles holding the breast collar, then undid the cinch. Taking the saddle off and the bridle, he sent the mare trotting down the track. He tied the blanket, bridle

147

and collar to the saddle strings, took down Burleigh's rope, doubled it, then, as the big cowboy struggled to get up, he hurled the saddle over his back.

"Now," Lee snapped. "You're going to pretend you're a horse and pack that heavy saddle back to your place of business. Every time you slow down, Burleigh, I'm going to use this rope on your fat butt and show you just what it feels like to your horse to be whipped!"

The beaten cowboy struggled to his knees, blood still streaming from his nose, and half turned as though to throw off the saddle and take up the fight once more.

Whap! The stiff, doubled nylon cut Burleigh across the wallet pocket, and the big man went to his knees in pain.

"Now get up and gallop," the boy commanded.

Beaten, Burleigh hoisted the saddle across his shoulders, clutching a D ring in each hand, and began to walk back toward the encampment.

Whap! Once more the rope caught him across the seat of the britches. "When I say 'gallop'," Lee said, "I mean 'gallop'!"

There were half a hundred cowboys cheering along the track by the time Ruff Burleigh came staggering in packing his saddle; and every time he tried to slow down, Lee unloosed the rope on him again.

Slim Pickens sat on his pinto mule, Judy, his round face split into a big grin. He wasn't at all sure what had taken place out there on the track that morning, but he knew there had been a happening that would become part of rodeo history, and that the scrawny kid from the slums, Lee Overalls, had become a man.

chapter
twenty-two

❖

The police checked him out again at noon. Lee sensed that they were merely fishing for clues to the thefts and had little to go on. Since last night, he had more reason than ever to hope Maroncita didn't find out about his past. To him, however, his past was like a shed snakeskin, of little concern to the snake; what mattered most was what he was now. Slick had been in control of several young lives; for any of them to stand up against him would have meant certain beatings, and maybe more unexplained deaths in the crowded tenements.

He didn't expect to find Slick among the vendors today. If the thief had indeed been Slick, he would have moved on with his loot. Slick was like lightning, never striking twice in the same place. Just the same, Lee thought, he would watch those vendors, and he didn't need cops to do that.

From what the police let slip, he gathered that King Richards had been bad-mouthing him around the other contestants, but the folks who meant most to him were above gossip. Then too, most of the cowboys had known Ruff Burleigh a long time and were tickled that someone had given him a taste of his own medicine. Actually, as long as Pam, Maroncita, and Slim believed in him, nothing else mattered.

The police went off again about their business, advising him to stick around until after the rodeo was over.

He rode a bareback bronc halfway across the arena before he bucked off. He was having a hard time getting the hang of them. The other cowboys leaned way back and spurred high, but if he did that, he lost track of the animal. This time he lit hard and had the wind knocked out of him, but was relieved to find he hadn't broken any bones.

He helped Maroncita with her trick riding, taking that opportunity to watch the vendors carefully. There were six of them again today, all with trays of goods, all dressed in white outfits with beaked hats, designed to inspire confidence in the cleanliness of the food. He tried to get a good look at each face, but at that distance it seemed impossible.

He talked to Jack Spurling along the chutes and asked him point blank what he was doing wrong in the bareback riding. Jack wasn't very big, but on the deck of a bareback bronc or a bull he could be mighty. He smirked at Lee as though considering some flip answer, then wiped the shock of black hair out of his eyes and told Lee he'd noticed that the horse had caught his spur when he came forward with his shoulder and dragged him to one side. "You got long legs, cowboy," he said. "A little horse like that, you'd been better off puttin' a little kink in yer knees."

150

In the saddle bronc riding, Lee drew a big sorrel horse out of Canada called Snake.

Slim happened to know the horse. "Runs out there like yore goin' to rate a reride, then POW! He throws a couple of freak jumps I mean are somethin' else. Goes up so high yew need oxygen. He's like thet old Badger Mountain; most cowboys just plain don't like to get 'im in the draw."

If Lee hadn't been coached, Snake might have taken him by surprise and bucked him off. As it was, he managed to ride, and this time kept fourth place all to himself.

As Maroncita was putting on her makeup, he came in excited by his ride and kissed her so hard she had to start over. For one tiny second, she appeared angry, then her face softened in a smile.

"Better let an old lady tend her face," she said. "That audience out there hasn't paid good money to look at wrinkles."

When she was done, she slid over on the bench and let him sit beside her as he applied his greasepaint. She added a touch of carmine to the corners of his mouth. "There." She laughed. "Now you look sad. Folks like sad clowns."

"How can I look sad when I'm happy?" he said. "Happier than I've ever been before!"

For a moment she turned her lovely eyes toward him and regarded him, then turned away. Leaving the bench, she went to a rack of blouses. She tried one after another, holding each up in front of her as she looked in the mirror. Finally, she selected one of palest apricot, dropped her robe about her waist, and put it on, straightening the ruffles along her slim bare neck.

"You'll knock 'em dead!" Lee said, glowing with pride.

When she had finished dressing, they moved toward the

door. Lee took her carefully in his arms and regarded her with wonder. "You be careful," he ordered.

"You too, Lee." A cloud passed over her, and she blinked away what might have been a mist of tears. He wondered if she were thinking of another good-bye, years past, the day her husband was killed.

When they came out of the van together, Pam was riding toward them ahorseback. She looked at them for a moment, then reined her horse away and rode out alone on the track. Maroncita busied herself with her mares and didn't seem to notice the girl.

Lee set up the jump and held her horses for her, clowning a bit with the folks in the audience and flirting with a pretty girl his own age in the front row. But he kept track of the vendors.

The man he was most suspicious of was only thirty feet away, standing with his back toward the track. He had trouble making change, and one of his customers seemed to be arguing with him. The vendor gave a quick glance over his shoulder at Lee, then handed the angry man more money and moved off, climbing higher into the stands.

Lee pulled himself up over the railing and started after him. A harried father, hastening twin boys in cowboy hats toward the rest room, came down the steps, blocking the aisle. He smiled at the clown apologetically. The vendor was climbing faster now, ignoring customers on each side.

"Hi, Mister Overalls!" It was his friend of the day before. She had her little brother with her. "I told ya I knew him," she said to the boy.

Lee patted them both on their heads and went on climbing. The vendor had disappeared behind the huge trusses holding the roof. Lee began to run, taking the steps in giant strides.

He was too late. He ducked around a bulwark only to find a tray of brown paper bags and white popcorn boxes, sitting deserted on an empty bench. The vendor had gone over the back of the stands and down. One after another, Lee took the bags and boxes and tore them open. Peanuts and popcorn, nothing more.

He regretted not having gone to the police with his suspicions. He could have flushed the vendor right into their hands. Now he was spooked and wouldn't come back. The chance of King and Maroncita recovering their valuables seemed gone.

Today, he stayed out of the barrel, working as one of a team with Slim to protect the bull riders from being gored. Slim didn't seem to mind, and when one luckless rider bucked off with his hand still caught in the loose-rope, while Slim caped the bull sharply to the right, Lee dashed in from the left to jerk the cowboy free. Slim grinned at him. "Let me tell yew somethin' " he said to Lee. "Yew shore are catchin' on fast!"

When the Gray Ghost came out, however, and bucked his rider off, Slim sent Lee back to the barrel.

"Let's not waste this good barrel bull," Slim said. "He gets better every time."

The bull gave the barrel quite a hammering, and Lee began to wonder if there weren't better ways to make a living.

As he lay beside Maroncita that night, as close as two spoons, he stared off into the darkness and wished that he could tell her about the elusive vendor. But if he explained

153

his suspicions, he might have to reveal his past, and he couldn't quite handle that just yet. He decided to put it off for a better time.

The moonlight shone through the window of the van and made a soft, pearly aura around her face as she slept. He was too aware of her presence to relax. He heard King Richards come out of his trailer and walk past on his way to the stock pens to check his horses; then, some minutes later, he heard him return, opening and closing the door of his trailer.

But then, a half hour later, he heard something else: the scrunch of gravel again. Someone else had passed by heading for the stock pens.

Lee rose from Maroncita's side. She murmured softly, but did not wake. Barefoot, he crept to the window. Maybe King had forgotten something and gone back. But as he glanced over toward King's trailer, he saw the lights blink out. King had to be inside!

Slipping on his clothes and his sneakers, Lee opened the door of the van and slipped outdoors. The moon was bright, so he kept to the shadows and headed toward the pens. Ahead of him, he could see the ghostly figure of the vendor, carrying a bundle slung over one shoulder.

He heard Blackhawk snort in alarm, and the rest of the horses began to mill about the corral. The man in white stopped in his tracks and stood motionless, letting the horses settle down.

As Lee crept forward for a better look, the vendor set his bundle beside the fence, took a pitchfork and began cleaning hay from the mangers, dropping it back out of the corral, out of reach of the horses. When the mangers were clean, he hoisted his bundle up over the top rail and emptied it into the racks. He was feeding those horses something, but what? It didn't make any sense. If that was Slick, what on earth would he be doing around a stock corral at midnight?

Blackhawk snorted, laid back his ears and made a short rush, putting the man back over the fence. Lee crept closer; he had no weapon and his only chance to capture the man lay in surprise.

On Lee's right, several brahma cows were lying in a pen chewing their cuds. Suddenly one of the cows spooked, and the whole bunch followed her to her feet, piling up in first one fence corner, then the other. Lee hugged the fence, trying to hide behind a post.

He saw the vendor pick up his canvas and run, ducking around the corner of the horse corrals, to become lost in shadows. The boy heard the faint rattle of a gate latch, and the creak of hinges. The man must have let himself into the deserted arena.

Lee leaped the fence, charged past the milling cattle, and peered out into the arena from beneath the announcer's stand, fully expecting to see the man fleeing across the arena toward the grandstand. But there was no one there. In the moonlight the bullfighting barrel gleamed a ghostly red.

The barrel was canted a little to one side, and as he looked at it Lee thought he saw it shift slightly, then straighten. Now he understood! The vendor was hiding inside the barrel. No need to hurry now. He began to whistle aloud King Richards' favorite tune, "Across the Alley from the Alamo." If the person happened to be familiar with King's habits, he might figure King was fussing with his animals and would stay under cover in the barrel until he left the area.

He saw Blackhawk moving toward the manger to sniff the contents. Quickly he scrambled along the catwalk, grabbed armloads of the hay out of the manger and tossed them out of reach of the horses. Something rattled in his hand, and he felt a large, bladder-like leguminous pod. The hay was loco-weed!

Moving back over the catwalk, still whistling calmly, he peered out into the arena. The barrel had sprouted legs and moved a dozen feet out across the sand before settling down again.

In the pen below him, most of the brahma bulls were resting out the night calmly. But the Gray Ghost rose to his feet, shaking his horns, then pawed the ground and moved toward him. Lee climbed down the gate leading to the chutes, opened it, waved his hand at the bull, and teased him into following. As Lee leaped up the fence, the bull rattled the planks beneath his feet. In the arena the barrel had sprouted legs again and was moving toward the grandstand. Another twenty feet and it stopped, settled once more to the ground.

Lee moved the Gray Ghost into Chute Five and slammed the gate behind him, grabbed a flank off the fence and dropped it down on the bull, reaching through the slats beneath the Ghost with his arm, hoping the bull wouldn't choose that moment to kick. He tugged the flank snug, knowing it would slow the bull down and keep him from running off down to the end of the arena.

The monstrous animal shook his hump, rattled his horns against the planks, and tried to reach Lee through the slats, then began shifting back and forth, seeking a way out of the chute.

Whoever was in that barrel was rock still now and must be wondering what was about to happen.

Lee pulled the pin on the gate and the Gray Ghost moved out of the chute head high, front legs spread wide, looking for something to fight.

As the bull skidded to a stop eyeing the empty arena, Lee stepped out from behind the white gate. "Hey, Ghost," he said softly. "Here I am!" The bull saw him in the moonlight, lowered his head and boiled after him.

The young cowboy ran straight for the barrel and ducked behind it just as the bull hit. The barrel leaped into the air, then crashed a dozen feet away as the Gray Ghost followed it, driving it spinning across the arena with his horns. Lee kept running backwards, keeping the barrel between himself and the animal. Well out into the arena, the bull paused, pawing the ground, showering its hump with dirt. Its eyes gleamed murderously, and it sparred with its horns.

Lee eased the barrel upright and tilted the opening toward the beast, so that the man crouching in the barrel could look the bull full in the face.

"Now, Jimmy Richards," Lee said. "It's me, Lee Overalls! I've got you right where I want you. You see the horns on that bull? That's the Gray Ghost, Jimmy, your dad's best barrel bull. He can peel you right out of that barrel like flesh from a slip-skin grape. Take a look out, Jimmy. You're looking at Death. Death with a capital D! I'm going to let this bull knock you around a bit till you're silly, then I'll let him eat you right out of the barrel."

The Gray Ghost made a short rush, and just as Lee straightened the barrel up, the bull hit with a resounding whump! As the barrel hit the ground again, the bull ducked around it trying to get to the clown. Dodging the bull's charge, Lee put the barrel between them again and tipped it up, this time with Jimmy's feet in the air.

"Sorry about that, Jimmy." Lee grinned, righting it. Once more he tipped the mouth of the barrel towards the bull. "Look at those eyes, Jimmy! He's a killer, that one!"

"Lee!" Jimmy whined. "Hey, old buddy, get that bull the hell away from me. Please!"

Lights were beginning to show among the trailers in the encampment. Good. No use performing without an audience. The bigger the better.

Jimmy was retching now in fear. Lee teased the Ghost into hitting the barrel a savage chop, and the horns drummed against the sides with a rapid tatoo. "There's one for killing your poor old dog, Bum."

"You don't understand, Lee! The damn dog attacked me! He wouldn't let go!"

The bull struck again and sailed the barrel high into the air. When it lit, Jimmy's legs trailed out on the ground, and the bull caught his trouser leg with one splintered horn and ripped it open.

"Better tuck your legs up, Jimmy. I don't want you to die too soon."

Lee righted the barrel as the bull put his nose over the top and drooled a great string of saliva across Jimmy's ear.

"You tried to frame me, Jimmy. You knew when you stole your dad's tack and Maroncita's things it would all be blamed on me."

"Lee! Let me off. Please, Lee. I needed money real bad! I'll split with you, honest I will!"

Jimmy tried to look up out of the barrel to see Lee's face, but the bull saw motion and charged again, sending the barrel spinning; in the process, he nearly knocked Lee down.

Close, Lee thought. *It sure wouldn't do to get myself hurt right now!*

"There's once more, Jimmy, for feeding locoweed to your dad's horses."

"He hated me," Jimmy whined, " 'cause he knew I was

scared. He wanted me to be a champion just like him. He kicked me out when I wouldn't ride, an' throwin' his horses off their feed an' slowin' them down was the only way I had of gettin' even. Woulda taken lots more locoweed than just one feeding to make 'em crazy."

Lee could see faces now along the fence. Cowboys coming, and King Richards's booming voice. "What the hell's goin' on here?"

"You don't want to know," Lee replied.

He saw Slim Pickens running toward him, barefoot and bare chested, clad only in trousers. "Lee! Is thet yew? Whut in thunderation are yew doin' out here fightin' bulls by moonlight. Yew think yore Tyrone Power in *Blood and Sand?*"

Lee smiled at Slim. "Jimmy Richards is taking a shot at being a barrel man," he said. "He's the one who's been doing the stealing around here. And he filled the manger in the saddle bronc pen with locoweed, too."

"I'll be danged," Slim said. "Whatcher goin' tew do with 'im?"

There was the sound of retching from the barrel. "Slim! Slim! Don't let 'im kill me!"

"I'm going to let this bull eat him, Slim, unless he wants to tell us where he's stashed the loot."

"It's in a motel," the cowboy sobbed. "I got the key hid under a footing over at the grandstand. I was afraid of getting caught with it on me. I'll take you to it. Please let me go!"

The Grey Ghost seemed to sense that they were through with him and went trotting off to stand at the far end of the arena.

Slim helped the boy out of the barrel, and Jimmy stood there facing his father.

159

"Jimmy!" King Richards said. "My son! Yuh gave loco-weed to my horses, tryin' tuh put me out of the rodeo business? Yuh must hev hated yore old man like hell!"

He didn't wait for an answer, simply walked to the stricken youth and put his giant arms around him.

"Lee," King Richards said. "I reckon we've caused yuh a lot o' grief. We'll mek it up tuh yuh any way we can."

chapter twenty-three

Maroncita was still asleep when Lee crept back to bed. Before drowsing off, he lay for a few moments staring up into the darkness, thinking that suddenly life was good again. When he awoke, daylight had already flooded the van.

He arose, dressed, and slipped outside, took care of the mares, and headed out on the track. A couple of cowboys who had never before been friendly greeted him with grins and joined him, but they couldn't stand his restless pace and fell behind. His friend the meadowlark was there again, singing in pure liquid, ecstasy as he moved on by. Pam came loping up from behind and passed him, showering him with clods, but she didn't even nod.

"I wonder," Lee thought, "if anyone really understands girls? Why didn't she stop her mare and have it out with me, get rid of that anger she's packing on her back?" He watched as she disappeared around the bend of the track and kept on running. After a shower, he went to the van for breakfast. King had returned Maroncita's possessions while he was jogging, and the art objects were already back on their shelves as though they had never been away.

"You had a busy night," she said, smiling at him as she gave him a hug. "They're going to let Jimmy off the hook this time," she added. "I didn't feel like pressing charges, and King feels he's partially to blame. No more rough stock for Jimmy; he's going to stay home and run King's ranch."

"Pam," he said. "She's mad at me. I guess it's because you and I are together. Won't even speak."

Maroncita nodded. "Shes angry with me, too." She looked at Lee as though she wanted to say something that was heavy on her mind, but turned away to fix his breakfast.

"I drew a saddle bronc called Doc Depression," Lee said. "Slim thinks if I manage to ride him, I'm a cinch to make the finals."

"That would be nice," Maroncita said. She busied herself with her costumes, and when Lee finished his coffee, he went out. He kept watching for Pam, intending to make her talk to him, but she was nowhere to be seen.

He sat on a bale of hay, relaxing with some of the other contestants. Cecil Henley, the nice old cowboy from California, showed him how to braid a buck rein, and he sat with the makings dead-ended on the trailer hitch of someone's pickup truck and practiced braiding. If Pam wanted to make up, he wanted to be there where she could find him. He missed having her always at his elbow. She was full of beans, that girl, always making him smile with her outrageous comments. He hoped she wouldn't stay mad long.

He was glad when the rodeo started. This time he managed to ride his bareback bronc, though he didn't score nearly

162

as well as the horse. He put a little kink in his knees the way Spurling had suggested, and it seemed to help.

Pam made another perfect run in the barrel racing, and for the third straight day, led the pack. He wished that she would come and sit beside the bucking chutes with him and watch the other contestants, but she rode out of the arena, put her horse away, and vanished.

He made a good ride on Doc Depression. Just a few weeks ago, the horse might have seemed difficult to him, but not now. "A pussy cat." He grinned at Slim as he passed him on his way back to the chutes. "Plumb gentle, that one."

As Slim had predicted, he made the finals. He sat on the fence and listened to the names as they drew them out of the hat. "Stub Bartlemay—Yellow Fever. Cecil Henley—Mastadon. Ross Dollarhide—Battle Mountain. Bill Linderman— Blue Blazes. Bill McMacken—High Desert. Lee Overalls— Blackhawk!"

He didn't mention the finals or Blackhawk to Maroncita. He helped her with a few chores, then went down to the saddle bronc pens and stood quietly at the big animal's shoulder. He wished they'd discover a mistake somewhere, that they'd added the points wrong, and that he wasn't even in the finals. Then someone else would have to try to ride the big black outlaw.

He went over to the stands then, leading Maroncita's tandem team. It was her last King Richards performance of the season, and they were planning to go south through Wyoming and Yellowstone, then on to Idaho and the big one at Pendleton. She rode as though she wanted to impress King Richards, so that he'd carry the memory of her final performance through the next few months to the time when he started thinking about next year's contracts.

163

Lee led her horses back to the van, and when he had tied them up, she took his hand and drew him inside the door where it was private and kissed him long and tenderly.

"Lee," she said. "Whatever happens, I want you always to remember one summer in Montana."

It was soon time to get ready for the finals. Slim refused to let him fight bulls, claiming he needed to save his strength for Blackhawk. Lee caught the horse up himself and led the big black into the proper chute to be saddled. Once the horse was ready, he sat quiet and relaxed on the chute gate, watching each rider in the finals do his own personal thing, and tried to learn from it.

"Git ready, Lee," Slim said. "Hey, yew know what? I got a feelin' yew can ride this old horse an' win this show fer sure."

As Lee settled down upon Blackhawk's back and found the stirrups, the big black turned his head and looked back at him. Lee fiddled with his rein, trying to remember how he'd measured it off when he'd come out before. He found a spot that felt good and nodded to the gate man. "Let's have him!" he said.

The last thing he remembered as he left the chute was Mel Lambert's voice announcing Lee Overalls, on the great bucking horse Blackhawk, an outlaw that "had never been rode."

Blackhawk soared out of the chutes in a power dive, then went to bucking fast and dirty, sunfishing, fence-railing, swapping ends, throwing his massive head, standing first on one end, then the other.

"Ride 'im, Lee!" Slim Pickens screamed.

Lee caught the rhythm when there was one. In all the world at that moment there was just himself and this magnificent athlete of a horse. The saddle jerked crazily between his knees as he spurred. It was as though Blackhawk had copied the best moves of some great horses. The head-slinging of Sceneshifter, the back kick of Miss Klamath, the wild show-stopping upredictability of Steamboat, the rearing plunge of Badger Mountain, and the spirit of Five Minutes Till Midnight!

One! he counted. *Two, three, four, five!* Every time the big black smashed the ground it seemed to knock another number out of Lee. *Six!*

The crowd was already on its feet roaring in applause. History was being made. Blackhawk, that great unridable saddle bronc, was about to be conquered by a slim, brave newcomer to rodeo, Lee Overalls.

Seven! Eight! I've got it made, Lee thought. One more great sunfishing leap! Blackhawk turned on his side in mid-air, fell earthward, then caught himself, but the boy stuck like a burr.

"Nine!" In that brief instant, as the horse soared again, the boy stepped hard in his right stirrup, doubled his left leg, threw the rein high in the air, and stepped out into space. When the whistle blew, he had solid ground under his feet.

He looked at Mel Lambert in the announcer's stand and grinned. Mel would understand. And Slim. Let someone else ruin the old horse's reputation. It wasn't going to be him. Winter was coming up; maybe the old horse would go to his reward without ever having been conquered!

As he left the arena, he heard Mel's voice booming out over the arena. "Ladies and gentlemen. Whatever history may choose to say about this occasion, I'm sure that everyone who was here today will agree that we say a young bronc rider named Lee Overalls make one helluva ride!"

Lee walked slowly back toward Maroncita's van. He was

exhausted. No one said anything to him; they all seemed stunned. King Richards reached out and touched his hand, and Jimmy saluted him in silent admiration. Slim sat on the fence beside his wife Maggi, both of them at a loss for words.

Lee saw Pam sitting on her horse, her face looking like death warmed over. He unbuckled his chaps, draped them over one shoulder and journeyed on. Past the stock corrals, Lee looked thoughtfully at the ground as he walked, smiling a little now, knowing that he'd done the right thing.

There was something wrong up ahead. He looked for Maroncita's big brown van and couldn't find it where he had left it. His head swam. There was King Richards's trailer, and the fence where the mares had been tied. Maroncita's van had moved out, leaving only tire tracks in the dust and a few flattened blades of grass where the wheels had pressed the earth. His bedroll and his meager possessions were piled neatly on a ground sheet, resting in the dust where once his happiness had been.

He heard Maroncita's voice then and words he would remember all his lifetime. "Whatever happens, I want you always to remember one summer in Montana."

A spring chinook blew in from the south, melting the snows, and sending streams of pale meltwater booming down the canyons. Lee Overalls clucked softly to the big team of matched roan draft horses, and they leaned into their collars, tightening the tugs, pulling the wagon load of loose hay out over the bare hillside. On the brow of the bald hill above him, Blackhawk stood watching for a moment, then led his bunch of retired rodeo broncs down toward the feed ground.

As the team plodded on, Lee took his pitchfork and began rolling hay over the side of the wagon. Among the timothy,

166

the clover smelled sweet as summer. Blackhawk nickered to him and came up alongside the wagon, following along to lick up seed from the bare planks where the hay had lain. At twenty-five, the big black looked good, ready for the rodeos, but King had elected to turn him out to pasture to live out his life in retirement, undefeated.

Lee's right leg was in a walking cast. He'd broken it during the last rodeo of the season, but it had healed well during the winter. The cast was due off in another week, and he was looking forward to making the first rodeo of spring. The last few weeks he'd been trying out on some practice broncs, and even with his foot in the cast, King and Jimmy both said they had never seen him ride better.

When the hay was fed off, he took the reins and turned the team back toward the barn. Heading home, the team wanted to prance a little, but he held them in. Life was good and life was full. He could feel the warmth of the sun through his winter coat. As he glanced down at the log ranch house set among the cottonwoods, he saw Pam come out of the front door and scan the hillside, one hand shading her eyes against the sun. She waved to him; he waved back, and the team began to hurry.